392A

EXX⊛ON-ERATION

RICHARD ROHMER

EXXON-ERATION

McClelland and Stewart Limited

0-7710-7702-5

The Canadian Publishers
McClelland and Stewart Limited
25 Hollinger Road, Toronto

Printed and bound in Canada by
T. H. Best Printing Company Limited,

Books by Richard Rohmer

The Green North Mid-Canada (1970)
The Arctic Imperative (1973)
Ultimatum (1973)

Special thanks to
John A. MacNaughton of Fry Mills Spence
for his technical advice

**To my mother
and my father**

October 6 & 7, 1980

On Monday morning, October 6, 1980, the President of the United States—a tough Texan fighting for re-election the next month—telephoned the new Prime Minister of Canada, Robert Porter, to deliver a harsh, unexpected set of demands for access to Canada's Arctic natural gas.

The conclusion of their one-sided discussion had led to the President's ultimatum.

After explaining that the United States was heading for a national disaster as a result of natural gas shortages, the President demanded three unconditional commitments from the Parliament of Canada. First, Canada had to settle the problem of aboriginal rights which had been holding up the pipeline construction. The President's model for such a settlement was the one the United States had worked out with the native people of Alaska.

Second, the President demanded that Canada grant the United States full access to all the natural gas in the Arctic Islands without reference to Canada's future needs.

And third, he requested a commitment that the United States be allowed to construct a transportation system as quickly as possible from the Arctic Islands to the United States.

"I want these commitments by six o'clock tomorrow night," the President told Porter, "and they must be given by the Parliament of Canada, not simply the government."

The Prime Minister acted quickly. Parliament was called for an emergency session, and by 5:00 P.M., October 7, both the House of Commons and the Senate had unanimously rejected the ultimatum. Instead, they proposed a conciliatory resolution, expressing a desire to negotiate with the native peoples of the Yukon and the Northwest Territories and with the government of the United States, but not without taking into account the future needs and requirements of Canada.

At 5:25 P.M., in the afternoon of October 7, 1980, just slightly more than a half hour before the expiry of the President's ultimatum, the Prime Minister officially informed the President of Parliament's decision. The President refused to tell the Prime Minister what his next step would be. The Prime Minister would have to wait until 6:30 that evening, he said, when he would advise the American people of the action of the Canadian Parliament and his decision on the matter.

The Prime Minister then went to Government House to be with his friend and longtime mentor and now Governor-General, Alexander Sinclair, to await the President's television statement.

The two of them watched and heard the President with apprehension. As he drew to the end of his speech, the President explained that he did not want the Canadian people to suffer as a result of the Canadian government's selfish decision, and wished to avoid the confrontation that would result if economic sanctions and counter-sanctions were put into force.

"As of this moment," he announced, "Canada will become a part of the United States of America." The government of Canada was to be dissolved, and the provinces to become states of the Union. After explaining that to ensure this annexation he had ordered transport aircraft

8

and helicopters of the United States Air Force to all major Canadian cities and Armed Forces bases, he went on to bestow upon the people of Canada citizenship in the "proudest, finest, greatest nation in the world"–the United States.

The Governor-General and Prime Minister Porter had sat in stunned silence throughout this speech.

"Well, Bob," the Governor-General sighed, touching Porter lightly on the arm, "it appears we have no choice. We fought for our independence as long as possible, but it couldn't last. My last act as Governor-General must be to follow the instructions of the President."

Ottawa
Tuesday, October 7, 1980, 6:38 P.M.

The Prime Minister leaped to his feet. "No! There is no goddamn way we're going to surrender, sir." He walked quickly to the telephone which was already ringing. Before he picked it up, he turned to the Governor-General and said, "This is exactly what we expected them to do if they were going to do anything military, and we're ready for them."

Before the Governor-General could express his surprise, Porter picked up the telephone and said, "Porter here."

At the other end was the Chief of Defence Staff, General Adamson.

"Sir, the Americans are committed to land. Their lead aircraft are on their final landing approaches right across the country – Dorval, Toronto, Vancouver, Edmonton, Halifax – the whole bit."

The Prime Minister's response was instant. "Okay, General, Operation Reception Party is GO."

Toronto
Tuesday, October 7, 1980, 5:15 P.M.

Colonel Pierre de Gaspé, commander of the Toronto District of the Canadian Reserves land forces, reached quickly for the ringing phone on his Fort York Armouries desk as it rang. He was expecting this call.

"De Gaspé here."

It was, as he expected, the commander of the Mobile Command, Lieutenant General Christie, at the Canadian Forces Base, St. Hubert, Quebec.

"Pierre, it's Christie. As briefed, Operation Reception Party will be mounted immediately. Parliament has just rejected the American ultimatum, so God knows what's going to happen next. I hope Reception Party turns out to be an academic exercise for all of us."

"So do I, sir," de Gaspé responded. "I might tell you that the response of the Reservists of the Toronto garrison has been incredible. We have every man and woman out who can move, and the British troops are just as up as we are."

"I'm not surprised," said Christie. "As you know, the Prime Minister must give the President Canada's answer by six o'clock. If the Americans take the military action against us, we calculate they'll start at us some time this evening. I can't believe they will, but they might. The Prime Minister and the Chief of the Defence Staff both are of the strong opinion that the Americans will go for economic sanctions but the possibility of an attack is obviously one we have to be prepared for. It's now seventeen fifteen hours. What's the status of your deployment."

De Gaspé's response was immediate. "We're set to go, sir. We've been in position at the airport since four-thirty. We moved our vans and jeeps independently, rather than in convoy, so we wouldn't get the public panicking. My artillery people have done an excellent job picking out the hidden locations for their guns around the edge of the airfield, and the ground-to-air missile people are deployed so they have clear shots at aircraft on the ground or in the air. Everybody's in place and my chopper's across the street waiting for me."

"Great stuff, Pierre. Our communications net is now locked in so you and I can be in constant touch. If you need decisions, you can get me instantly. Away you go."

As he put the receiver down, Pierre de Gaspé's mind went back to the staggering briefing he and the other district commanders from across Canada had received that morning in Ottawa where they had all been summoned on an emergency call from the Chief of the Defence Staff.

As a Reservist and as the man responsible for the Toronto Militia District, Colonel de Gaspé had moved into full-time command the day before, immediately the news was out that the President of the United States had given the ultimatum to the Prime Minister. Even before the mobilization signal had been received from National Defence Headquarters, de Gaspé had left his comfortable office in the new Metro Centre complex. In his civilian capacity as president of Petro-Canada and one of the most experienced and knowledgeable petroleum industry executives in Canada, he had been expecting an ultimatum to be delivered by the United States as its natural gas shortages escalated to crisis proportions. Now his fears had been realized in a scale and with a ruthlessness no one could have expected from, of all nations, the United States.

The briefing had taken place at 9:15 A.M. on the second day of the ultimatum period. It was held in an auditorium in National Defence Headquarters and had been given by the Chief of the Defence Staff himself.

The entire room had stood as General Adamson, an athletic-looking man of medium height, entered and proceeded to his position in front of the projection screen. He placed his papers on the lectern and asked the assembly to be seated.

He scanned the auditorium, filled with senior Regular Force and Reserve officers brought in overnight from across the country. He proceeded directly to the point.

"Gentlemen, as you are all aware, the President of the United States has delivered a three-part ultimatum to the Prime Minister of Canada. That ultimatum must be answered by the Parliament of Canada by six o'clock this evening.

"Just before noon yesterday I was instructed by the Prime Minister to call out the Reserves and to mobilize the Canadian Armed Forces to the fullest possible degree. This has been done, as is evidenced by the presence here of the Reserve District Militia commanders from all the major cities across Canada–and by the Air Reserve and Naval Reserve commanders.

"The government has directed that the Canadian Armed Forces be mobilized for two reasons. The first is that should there be raids or demonstrations which are anti-American and which might turn into physical violence requiring control, then the military will be available to aid the civil power, that is to say, the police, in containing such action. At the same time, the government is anxious that the military presence not be shown to the public unless and until absolutely necessary. Therefore, I have instructed all of you by signal, and I repeat it now, that all troops must be lodged inside the local armouries. They are not to venture out unless and until ordered.

"The second but most important purpose for mobilization is that the Prime Minister has instructed me that the Canadian Armed Forces must be prepared to meet any attack mounted by the United States against Canada, should the Parliament of Canada refuse the ultimatum."

With that there was much scuffling in the audience, the passing of whispered comments, and the rolling of eyeballs upwards.

General Adamson had expected this sort of reaction and waited a moment till his people settled down. He ran his hand through his thick greying hair. Then he took both sides of the lectern in his hands and continued.

"Gentlemen, let me tell you something. This Prime Minister of ours is one tough son-of-a-bitch. His instructions to me are very simple. There is no goddamn way the Americans are going to take over Canada without one hell of a fight!"

With that the room burst into spontaneous applause. The CDS beamed with pleasure at the response and went on. "The Prime Minister expects that if the ultimatum is rejected, the Americans will resort to economic sanctions rather than military force. On the other hand, the Americans look on our resources as being their own. They've put their money into them. They look on us as being weak-kneed, grey-faced people and they see our country as a colony of the States. Their attitude will probably be, 'Why not just take over Canada. After all, they've only got 50,000 people in the Regular Force and 35,000 in the Reserves. That should be peanuts so far as the giant American military machine is concerned.' They can see us sitting here with only five fighter squadrons, no bombers, no rockets, no ballistic missiles, no nuclear warheads. Nothing. A half-assed military force. At least that's what they think.

"Well, let's look at the facts. Our Regular Force is far too small. Our hardware–aircraft, tanks, guns, anti-tank and anti-aircraft weapons–are about one-tenth of what we should have. We're in that position because the Canadian people and their leaders decided and they decided some time ago, that this is the way it was going to be and that military expenditures were to be reduced and kept small.

"At the beginning of the 1970's almost all risk of war had disappeared, at least as between the major powers. People in government had no background in war or the military and were mainly concerned with social and cultural problems. They had little time or money for the military. They were brassed off with the Vietnam thing and what they saw there, even though that was strictly an American show.

"Well, the result is that if we have to take on the Americans, we haven't got much to do it with. In fact, we've got damn little."

His hand went through his hair again.

"Now, the fact that we've got little and the Americans recognize it, is the basis for our strategy and tactics in meeting this potential threat. And I can tell you, gentlemen, that it is my considered opinion as a military person that the Americans are going to bite the bullet and go for taking over Canada."

The CDS waved his hand toward the collection of sitting generals to his left and right.

"The Defence Staff and I have kicked this whole thing around from top to bottom. We think the Americans are going to take a look at us and say, 'There's no way these people are going to fight. They've got nothing to fight with, they're just a grey-faced bunch of people with a banana-republic military force. If we tell them to lay down their arms, that's exactly what they're going to do. So there's not going to be any need to send fighter or bomber aircraft to whip the hell out of them, or to bomb their cities. Furthermore, if we bomb or strafe, we'll probably be destroying U.S.-owned factories, office buildings, oil refineries – you name it. So we'll just tell the Canadians we're coming and then we'll walk in.'

"In fact, for the last twelve hours that's exactly the message we've been giving the Americans, just to lead them into the position of thinking we're going to be patsies. If they thought for one second we were going to take them on, they'd set up their strategy and tactics quite differently.

"Our analysis goes this way. If the Americans attack us in force with fighters, bombers, and troops shooting from the hip, we're going to be in real trouble because we just haven't got the capability of meeting them. On the other hand, if they are sensitive to world opinion – God knows whether they are or not – and if they think we're going to be pushovers and they can move in without firing a shot, then we've got a real chance to catch them by the shorts.

"Therefore, we've built our operational plan, called 'Operation Reception Party,' on the thesis that the Americans are going to think they can walk, ride, and fly in.

"If my analysis is correct, then how will they do it?

"First, they will mount an air assault by lifting in their men by using Starlifters, Hercules, and other large troop-transport aircraft, including helicopters. They will land at all major Canadian civilian and military airports, and they will be expecting absolutely no military resistance for the reasons I've given you. Also, they'll expect to take us by surprise.

"Second, no bombing or strafing will take place because of the likelihood of damage to American investments in Canada and possible injury or death for American nationals resident in or visiting this country.

"Third, there will be no advance attack by paratroopers

because that effort will be judged unnecessary by the politicians, even though their use will be recommended the the Pentagon.

"Fourth, ground troops, personnel carriers, and tanks will simultaneously attempt to move across the border.

"Gentlemen, if I were the Chairman of the United States Joint Chiefs of Staff this is how I'd read Canada, and this is how I would obey the President's instruction to invade.

"Each of you will now be handed a copy of the operation order for Operation Reception Party. The first thing you'll note is that I've decided to leave the Reserve District commanders in charge of the operation at Montreal, Toronto, and Winnipeg. It's too late to try to plug Regular Force people in. And the District commanders will report directly to the Commander of Mobile Command." He pointed toward the hefty, dark-haired Lieutenant General Christie on his immediate left.

"As you read the order one of the things you should add is that 1,200 British troops—two battalions—of the 15th Parabrigade will be arriving early this afternoon from the U.K. by arrangements made between our Prime Minister and the British Prime Minister last night. They'll be going into Canadian Forces Base, St. Hubert—just southeast of Montreal—CFB Downsview at Toronto, and at London, Ontario. Some of them will be moved into the Windsor sector. They will be under the command and control of the local District commanders.

"And now to the mechanics of Operation Reception Party."

17

Pierre Thomas de Gaspé

Colonel Pierre Thomas de Gaspé, a tall man with an easy smile and a domineering, forceful presence, was well suited to his temporary role of a military commander placed in a position of enormous emergent responsibility.

His father, Simon de Gaspé, had been a well-to-do Montreal lawyer, from an élite Quebec family. In 1941, shortly before his son's birth he had gone overseas as a captain of Les Fusiliers Mont-Royal Regiment, the FMR's. On August 19, 1942, he died on the beach of Dieppe, without ever seeing his son.

Simon's legacy of military and legal aspirations and examples had been strong motivating forces in the shaping of the life and career of his son. Pierre's mother, a delicate but strong-willed little woman from the wealthy, influential Thomas family of London, Ontario, had remained in Montreal until 1952, during which time Pierre received his education in French at the hands of excellent Jesuit teachers.

That year his mother had married a Toronto consulting economist and academic. This union brought her and Pierre to Toronto where the young boy continued his secondary school education with priests, this time with the Basilian Fathers at St. Michael's College.

He was raised with mother tongues of both French and English and with a soul and spirit saturated with each of the founding cultures and languages of Canada.

In 1960, at age eighteen, he entered the Royal Military College at Kingston, where he excelled in all aspects of his military and university training, graduating at the top of his class in engineering with sufficient economics credits from Queen's University to allow him to go on to obtain his Masters in Economics at that university, then to Harvard for his doctorate.

Early in his university studies, de Gaspé became intrigued by the relationship and importance of energy to the existence and maintenance of civilization. Eventually he concentrated on energy with particular reference to fossil fuels—crude oil and natural gas with their multitude of derivatives.

His masters thesis, written in 1963, on "Canada's Trade Prospects in the World Energy Shortage Crisis of the late 1970's" had shaken the Dean of the School of Economics, who found it impossible to believe that there could be such a thing as a world energy shortage, let alone one that would hit Canada. Nevertheless, the Dean recognized de Gaspé's brilliance as a student and envied his ability to deal with forward-looking concepts.

He had been so impressed that he sent the paper to the business editor of the Toronto *Globe and Mail*. The editor was also impressed and published major sections of Pierre de Gaspé's work in series form.

These articles caused an enormous amount of discussion at the Petroleum Club in Calgary. Many heated debates over de Gaspé's opinions took place over long liquid lunches and strenuous dinners. Thus at the age of twenty-two, de Gaspé was already causing controversy in the oil and gas industry in Canada. It was only the beginning of such disturbances.

At Harvard, he produced his doctoral thesis on "The Fossil Fuel Vulnerability of the United States and the

Urgent Requirement for Plans for Energy Self-Sufficiency," a paper which found its way in part into pages of the *New York Times* Sunday edition. With the publication of his work in that prestigious newspaper, Pierre de Gaspé established the beginnings of his credentials as a knowledgeable commentator on the economics of oil and natural gas in relation to the future requirements of the North American continent.

When he completed his work at Harvard in 1966, he was approached by several American oil corporations. The best offer was from Standard Oil of New Jersey, later known as Exxon. De Gaspé was at the top of their selection list from among all the bright young Ph.Ds emerging from American universities that year. But he was uncertain as to whether he should go directly into the oil industry. What he had in his mind was a law degree, not only because of his desire to follow in the path of the legendary father he had never known, but also because he could see that members of the legal profession occupied most of the chairs of power in big business in America and that lawyers generally had an enormous amount of flexibility. When he had talked about going on to law, his mother had chided him in a joking way about becoming a "professional" student.

In the end, after much discussion with and solicitation by the Standard Oil people, de Gaspé joined their corporate planning division as an economist. At the head office in New York, he spent the most intensive year of his life examining, probing, forecasting, analyzing, guessing, prophesying, and above all, learning about the intricate, complex, globe-encircling network of power that rested with a handful of the top executives of this largest of multinational oil companies, a firm of staggering wealth, virtually a nation unto itself.

De Gaspé soon became the protégé of the senior vice-president, George Shaw, and his wife Janet. They were both originally Canadians, and felt a kinship for this young man, even though they had long since become United States citizens. Through their almost parental interest in him, Pierre had been invited to many cocktail parties and dinners. In this way he had quickly broadened his association with both the young and the senior executives in the head office group.

Within a few months, de Gaspé had become a protégé part of the executive "family" of Standard Oil of New Jersey. The brilliance of his work was the cause of mounting admiration and respect for him. Promotion within his section came and with it a substantial raise.

But he was a man who kept looking ahead – where was he going, what was he doing, what were the prospects?

Within a year after he had joined Standard Oil, de Gaspé had made up his mind that, even though the attractions at Standard were enormous and the future looked to be incredibly good for him, he should take his law degree – but in Canada, not in the United States. He discussed the situation with Shaw in order to seek his advice and also to assess what the prospects would be for his return to Standard Oil when the law degree was behind him. Shaw tried to dissuade him, telling him what the future could hold if he stayed inside Standard. But Shaw's discouragement was only half-hearted because he knew if Pierre had his law degree that that professional qualification, combined with this young man's superior ability in economics, would enable him to call his own shots if he wished to return to Standard. He was frank and direct with de Gaspé. By the end of their talk, he had reversed himself.

In the late summer of 1968, de Gaspé packed his bags and, after a round of farewell parties and dinners, departed the head office of Standard Oil of New Jersey and headed for Montreal and the McGill University. The next three academic years were heavy with study of both Common Law and the Civil Code and in both French and English, with some of his courses being taken at Laval University. De Gaspé had headed his class and at the conclusion of the intensive law course was awarded the Gold Medal for academic achievement.

During his law studies, he spent his summer months in Toronto in the economic planning division of the head office of Imperial Oil, the Canadian subsidiary of Standard Oil of New Jersey. Working with Imperial did two things for him: it provided him with sufficient money to carry through the next academic year, and it allowed him to up-date his knowledge of the world oil, natural gas, and energy scene. He was also able to maintain his public visibility by continuing to write incisive, important papers which were published and commented upon in the petroleum industry's magazines and periodicals. These publications earned him some extra money, as did the occasional speaking engagements at various conferences and meetings. He had, however, no urgent need of money; he had been the beneficiary of two substantial bequests, one from his father's mother, who had died in 1959, and another from his father's own estate, the capital of which came to him when he turned twenty-one.

After graduating from McGill Law School and completing his Bar Admission course in Ontario in 1972, Pierre de Gaspé once again received several offers, but only two interested him. The first was from Shaw of Standard Oil of New Jersey which had changed its name to Exxon Corporation on January 1 of that year. Shaw, who had moved up to the position of executive vice-president and the number two man in the entire organization, wanted de Gaspé to be his executive assistant. He would be with him right at the top of Exxon and he would be paid accordingly. The opportunities for the future were unlimited. Pierre was mightily tempted, but he was certain that he did not want to live in the United States, nor would he give up his Canadian citizenship. He was apprehensive about the racial strife in the United States and the growing decadence of the once great American cities. Watergate was yet to be heard from but its roots had been silently planted and were flourishing.

The other offer – the one he accepted – was from Panarctic Oils Limited, then in its formative stages. Panarctic was a corporation put together in 1967 by the federal government of Canada, which took 45 per cent of its shares, offering the balance to Canadian and American oil corporations. The government had found that the oil companies operating in Canada were reluctant to make the high-risk and high-cost investment in exploration in the Arctic Islands, particularly in the Sverdrup Basin from Melville Island northeast to the Eureka area of Ellesmere Island.

When de Gaspé was approached by Panarctic, the company was at the beginning of a massive exploration program which was to prove enormously successful over the years, especially in the finds of natural gas on Melville at Drake Point at the beginning of 1970, King Christian Island later that year, then a whole series, not only on Melville and King Christian, also on Ellef Ringnes, Thor, Ellesmere, and other locations.

The money offered by Panarctic to join them as vice-president of economic planning and legal services was just slightly more than half of the Exxon bid, but de Gaspé was enthusiastic about the Panarctic's prospects in the Canadian Arctic Islands and about its ultimate potential as the national petroleum company. He could clearly foresee that such a company would be necessary if Canada was to deal with the Arabs, the South Americans, and other oil-producing countries around the world—nations that traditionally preferred to deal with governments or government companies. He could see Panarctic as the basic formation block for the future national petroleum company of Canada, provided it was successful in its exploration work in the Arctic. This condition was amply met within a short time after de Gaspé joined the firm at its head offices in Calgary in 1969.

In Calgary, Pierre had met and courted Ann Samson, a vivacious, petite medical doctor just finishing her internship at the Calgary General Hospital. Their marriage in 1970 was followed in 1971 by the birth of their son, Mark. Mark's godfather, George Shaw of Exxon, was thus on hand to celebrate another occasion in Pierre's life, when he was appointed senior vice-president of Panarctic, with a hefty salary increase and enlarged responsibilities in the exploration end of the firm's operation as well as in long-range planning and legal services.

During the mid-seventies, de Gaspé found himself in the middle of the escalating controversial debate between the federal government and the government of Alberta. He was seconded to Ottawa for a period of six months during the winter of 1974/75 to head up a team which would be responsible for laying out the ground rules and format for a continuing locked-in-until-it-was-finished conference between the federal government and the oil-producing and -exporting provinces. De Gaspé and other influential people in the oil industry had protested quietly but effectively to the federal government that a two-day first ministers "on camera" type of conference which had been held in January of 1974 was no answer whatsoever to the urgent need to resolve a whole series of questions related to what a national oil and natural gas policy should be. It was de

24

Gaspé's opinion that there should be a conference held on neutral ground away from Ottawa and that the participants should stay at it for weeks, if necessary, until they hammered out an overall set of principles under which the federal and provincial governments could operate in co-operation rather than confrontation. In early 1974, de Gaspé wrote a draft paper, "A National Energy Policy for Canada," in which he set out his policy proposals and his design for a Canada Energy Corporation.

Later in the year, the then Prime Minister read de Gaspé's paper, and he and the first ministers of the western oil and gas provinces agreed to use it as the starting point of the discussions in the conference.*

The great National Energy Conference, which took place in Winnipeg in the spring of 1975, went on for five weeks until all the major issues were resolved and new working arrangements were established under heads of agreement which were still effective and operative in 1980.

Immediately after the energy conference, the government had proceeded with the creation of a national petroleum corporation, which they called Petro-Canada. The corporation then acquired the government's interest in Panarctic and with it all its experienced personnel and all its wells, exploration rights, and know-how. De Gaspé was gratified to have his proposal put into action, but was appalled by the name Petro-Canada, which he detested.

The president of Panarctic, who had nurtured that firm from its beginning days and had done what was by and large regarded as an excellent job, was anxious to move away from the heavy responsibilities and constant travelling which he was finding exceedingly difficult to maintain.

And so, on the formation of Petro-Canada, Pierre

*Appendix I, page 204

25

Thomas de Gaspé became its first president and executive officer, and Panarctic's former president became chairman of the board. The head office of Petro-Canada was established in Toronto on an interim basis.

After his return to Toronto, the demands on de Gaspé's time almost doubled. He put his entire heart and soul into creating, shaping, and moulding this new national corporation. During the next five years, he spent a great deal of time travelling throughout Canada, the United States, Europe, and the Middle East. His wife Ann began to complain bitterly about his lack of time for his family. A strong-willed person, who by this time was having problems with her own identity, she began to spend more and more time in London, Ontario, with her mother.

By the summer of 1980, the relationship between Ann and Pierre had become distant, strained, and unhappy. Without consulting her husband, Ann made plans to take up her medical practice again, but this time in parternship with a young doctor with whom she had interned in Calgary. De Gaspé was furious when he found out, but powerless to do anything about it. When he met Ann's partner for the first time, he was even more upset. Dr. Rease was a strikingly handsome man, and a bachelor.

Notwithstanding this growing marital difficulty, de Gaspé's remarkable organizational ability, leadership, and intelligence had made Petro-Canada flourish as a combined free-enterprise/government undertaking, with de Gaspé marshalling new acquisitions and financings as he quickly spread the broad base of the new corporation to make it truly a national petroleum company.

But by the fall of 1980, he still had not been able to get Petro-Canada into the refining of crude oil and the wholesale and retail distribution of gasoline, fuel oil, and other petroleum products. For him, this was both a major objective and a source of frustration.

The fall of 1980 also provided Pierre Thomas de Gaspé with the most senior appointment of his military career, that of commander of the Toronto District of the land element of the Canadian Armed Forces Reserve, more easily recognized in Canada as the Militia.

When he had brought his family back to Toronto from Calgary in 1975, de Gaspé had accepted an invitation to return to his old Reserve unit, the Queen's York Rangers (1st American Regiment), as second in command with the rank of major.

He enjoyed his military hobby enormously. It gave him a much-needed recreational outlet and, at the same time, provided him a sense of satisfaction and fulfilment of the duty strongly embedded in his nature and background. By 1976 he had become commanding officer of the regiment with the rank of lieutenant-colonel, moving in 1979 as a full colonel to take the post of Toronto District Commander with all the Reserve regiments and other Militia units in the area under his command and control.

Thus, on the day of the President's ultimatum to the new Prime Minister of Canada, Pierre Thomas de Gaspé was wearing two hats, each of significant importance to Canada at that moment: the one as president of Petro-Canada which controlled and owned most of the natural gas in the Canadian Arctic Islands so desperately needed and coveted by the President of the United States; and the other as commander of the Toronto Militia District in a focal position of military responsibility. The hat of the energy executive had high public visibility, but that of the military commander, as is traditional in Canada in time of peace, was of little prestige or importance in a smug society which placed little value on its military establishment – except in an emergency.

On October 6, 1980, the emergency arrived.

Toronto
Tuesday, October 7, 1980, 6:10 P.M.

At noon, the Canadian government had closed the Canadian/U.S. border at all points where it physically could do so: these being the main points of traffic entry in the western provinces, the bridges at Sault Ste. Marie and Windsor/Detroit, and the tunnel there, the Peace Bridge at Fort Erie/Buffalo, the bridges at Niagara Falls and across the St. Lawrence.

Explosive charges were set in all of these structures so that a section but not all of the bridge or tunnel could be blown at the first sign of a military crossing from the American side.

At the same time, the Ministry of Transport ordered the closing down of all air traffic between the United States and Canada. By 6:00 in the evening when Operation Reception Party was in total readiness, there was absolutely no traffic into or out of any Canadian airport, big or small, except for military aircraft.

Telephone, telex, telegram, radio, and all other communications links with the United States were cut off at 3:00 P.M. The communications systems between the two nations had, however, been built without any planning for a shutdown situation, and considerable difficulties were encountered in this procedure.

All operatives of the CIA working in Canada were unobtrusively collected and taken to police or military headquarters for protective questioning.

Thus, while the House of Commons was in the last stages of its deliberation on the ultimatum question, an effective emergency shut-down of communications and transportation between Canada and the United States was being carried off as part of the plan of Operation Reception Party.

At the border-crossing points along the Great Lakes system, troops with machine guns, anti-tank weapons, and light artillery were in position in strategic locations overlooking the approaches to the lofting bridges. On a normal day they carried thousands of people, automobiles, buses, and trucks between two nations which, up to this moment, had lived side by side, divided only by an imaginary line – the longest, unprotected boundary between two nations in the Western world.

To the west of the Great Lakes, Operation Reception Party did not call for protection of the border crossings but the setting up of heavy roadblocks on each of the main highways between the border and the first major Canadian city to which each highway led. The roadblocks were approximately ten miles south of each urban objective. The Chief of the Defence Staff had calculated it would take the U.S. ground troops, personnel carriers, and tanks between one and two hours to reach the western roadblocks. By that time, the airports phase of Reception Party should be finished.

The scene at Toronto International Airport was typical of all major Canadian airfields. Air traffic had totally stopped by mid-afternoon following the Ministry of Transport order at noon. Both terminal buildings had been cleared of passengers and the lengthy ramps around the huge buildings were deserted of people and vehicles although jammed with parked aircraft.

Dispersed around the perimeter of the airport but in

locations that could not be seen by low-flying reconnaissance aircraft, troops equipped with missiles, machine guns, and artillery were in camouflaged positions at points overlooking the runways. Special priority had been given to the positioning of the light anti-tank TOW* missiles, the hand-held, short-range, surface-to-air Blowpipe missiles, and sophisticated British Rapiers, which were also surface-to-air missiles. They were to have a maximum opportunity for clear shots at incoming aircraft, both on the ground and in the air. It was these versatile weapons that would either make or break Operation Reception Party, if indeed the Americans decided to take the unthinkable military step.

Colonel de Gaspé's Kiowa helicopter hovered behind the control tower on the west side of the Toronto International, then gently touched down. His camouflage-net-covered command post vehicles were set up to the west of the control tower structure so that anyone in the air terminal building on the east side of the airfield would not be able to see them.

As the pilot eased the helicopter to the ground, de Gaspé pushed the VHF transmitter button on the control column in front of him and spoke into the microphone on his crash helmet.

"Toronto Tower. This is Reception leader. Over."

Toronto Tower came back, "Reception leader, Toronto Tower. Go."

"Right, Toronto Tower. Are you people all set as briefed?"

"Yes, sir, we sure are. If they come, we don't expect them to get any clearances from us until they're about twenty miles out. I don't expect they'll be getting air traffic control clearances, but we'll have no trouble painting them on our radar screens."

*TOW – tube-launched, optically tracked, wire-guided.

"Okay, Toronto Tower. We'll monitor your VHF control channels, and our communications net will monitor all normal military channels. We don't expect they'll have a communications security blackout. We think they'll do it wide open. Be with you in a couple of minutes."

"Roger. All your people are here waiting for you."

As de Gaspé swung himself out of the helicopter, he was met just outside the arc of the lift blades by his Regular Force staff officer, Lieutenant-Colonel Peter Armstrong, a tall, bear of a man for whom de Gaspé had developed an enormous respect since Armstrong had joined his staff that summer. De Gaspé regarded him as an enormously efficient soldier. He had graduated at the top of his class at Canadian Forces Staff College, commanded a section of the Canadian Airborne Regiment, seen combat service in Korea, and had taken part in the Canadian peace-keeping efforts in Cypress. What's more, Armstrong could drink even Pierre de Gaspé under the table, as he had proved on more than one occasion in mess dinners held from time to time by the various regiments and other units in the Toronto area.

Armstrong's hulking figure loomed even larger in his dark green camouflaged battle gear. His carbon blackened face completed his camouflage dress but looked a little amusing to de Gaspé who, as he returned Armstrong's salute, said, "Christ, Peter, you look like a goddamn grizzly bear."

Armstrong's great white teeth showed in a wide smile. "Thank you, sir. I thought you'd never notice."

As the two of them moved towards the control tower building and the command post truck parked directly to the west side of it, de Gaspé said, "Okay, Peter, give me a status report."

The sound of the helicopter engine died as the pilot cut off the power behind them. Men began to move toward the aircraft with camouflage nets.

"Yes, sir," Armstrong responded, "everything's in good shape. All units are in position. But I'd like to wait till we get up to the tower so I can point out to you where everyone is. The COs of all the regiments are there waiting for us. I thought if we had everybody together I could bring you up to date and then you could give us our final instructions."

Colonel de Gaspé took the stairs up to the control tower two at a time with Armstrong following close behind. As he entered the glass-walled control area, the battle-uniformed men, who seemed to fill the room with activity, chatting, and noise, came to military attention. Those with their helmets on saluted. De Gaspé returned the salute.

"Thank you, gentlemen," he said. "Stand easy."

His eyes swept across his team, making a fast inventory of who was there. Holoduke, commanding officer of the Queen's York Rangers; Purdy of the Queen's Own Rifles; Foy of the 48th Highlanders; Esplen of the Toronto Scottish; and Shepherd, the CO of the battalion of the crack British Parabrigade assigned to Toronto. The Brits, all 315 of them, had arrived an hour before in Hercules aircraft of the Royal Air Force Transport Command. They brought with them thirty-six of their new, highly accurate surface-to-air Rapier missile projectors with a supply of over five hundred missiles, a formidable arsenal to meet any air attack.

De Gaspé had been informed during the CDS's morning briefing that, because of the lack of time for preparation and also because of the need to spread them across the border-crossing roadblocks and the commercial and military airports in western Canada, the Alberta-based Canadian Airborne Regiment—the only available combat-ready mobile Regular Force unit—would have to be assigned exclusively to the western task. Therefore, virtually the entire defence of eastern Canada would be the responsibility of the Reserves, supported by whatever British troops would be shipped across in time.

De Gaspé introduced himself to Lieutenant Colonel Michael Shepherd, commander of the British unit.

"I can tell you, Colonel Shepherd, that I'm delighted to have you and your people on board."

Shepherd, a stocky, red-cheeked man in his early thirties, looked up at the much taller de Gaspé and smiled. "I think you're just interested in having our bloody Rapier missiles, sir."

De Gaspé laughed. "Now that you mention it . . . I haven't seen one in operation but I understand they're fantastically accurate, even on high-speed supersonic aircraft."

"That's right, sir. And on top of that, they have an excellent range. If we can see the target, we can hit it, whether it is one mile away or ten."

De Gaspé was impressed. "I understand Colonel Armstrong briefed you when you arrived?"

"Yes, sir. He brought me up to speed on the whole bit: what was happening in Parliament, the briefing you gave him and the Regimental commanders earlier this afternoon, the Defence Staff's analysis, the general strategy and tactics."

"Good," de Gaspé said. "I want to have a word with the air traffic controllers now, and then we'll get on with the final briefing." He smiled and put his hand on Shepherd's shoulder. "I'm delighted you're here, believe me."

Then he turned and introduced himself to the two air traffic controllers who identified themselves as Ray Walnek and Tom Spence. Both of them were obviously senior and highly experienced. Walnek was in charge.

"With the airfield shut down, I don't suppose you fellows have had it so quiet since your last strike." All three laughed together.

"I know Colonel Armstrong has briefed you, but I'd like to go over the plan with you myself, since you," de Gaspé nodded toward Walnek, "and I will be the main actors in receiving our American friends if, in fact, they do arrive."

With that, de Gaspé, Walnek, and Spence spent five minutes meticulously going over the role each would play should an American landing be in fact attempted. Walnek explained the functional workings of the VHF* radio equipment with which he controlled inbound and outbound aircraft and what de Gaspé was to do when it was time for him to interject as Walnek was dealing with the hypothetical incoming Americans.

In turn, de Gaspé made sure that Walnek and Spence knew how to use the military radio and communications equipment that had been set up in the tower.

"As Armstrong has told you, I plan to use the control tower as my command post," he said. "I want you to understand that all three of us will be highly vulnerable, because once I get on the air with my instructions to the lead American aircraft, the pilots will know I'm in the tower with you. Unless they have explicit instructions not to fire, they'll probably come in and attempt to take us out." Walnek and Spence looked at each other nervously. "I hope you're still game?"

"Sure, Colonel," Walnek responded. "Frankly, I don't think it's going to come off the way you think. I just can't see the Americans attacking us."

Spence nodded in agreement.

"I can't either," said de Gaspé. "But we've got to be prepared for the worst."

He then turned to Peter Armstrong. "Okay, Peter, let's get into the final briefing." Then, raising his voice, he

*VHF – very high frequency.

34

addressed the assembled men. "Gentlemen, we'll get on with the final briefing. Colonel Armstrong will brief me as to the deployment of your units. Don't hesitate to break in at any point with suggestions and questions. When he's finished, I will have a word or two, then you can get back to your people." He looked at his watch. "We haven't much time left. It's just after six. The President is scheduled to speak at six-thirty. My guess is if they're going to come after us, they're in their aircraft right now."

The men looked uneasily at each other. It was hard for any one of them to believe that this could be so.

"Okay, Peter. It's all yours."

Lieutenant Colonel Peter Armstrong began. "Right, sir. I've stuck up on the north window," he pointed, "a map of the airport. I will refer to it and indicate where our people are on the ground. Obviously, this control tower is perfect because we can see any part of the airfield from here.

"I'm only going to say, 'if they come' just this once, because the rest of my briefing will assume that they are coming. If they come, they'll be coming from the south, across the lake, probably from the southeast, south and southwest. The wind at this time is zero two zero at fifteen miles an hour and gusting, so they'll probably use the Runway 32–the longest. We don't know how many of them there'll be, but let's assume there are at least fifty. They'll want to get on the ground as quickly as possible and start unloading their troops as soon as they can get clear of the runway. The first aircraft will have to get quite a distance off before it stops, in order to let the incoming aircraft behind it have enough turnoff room."

He waved his right hand toward the Terminal One building, about half a mile to the east of the control tower.

"This airfield is designed so that aircraft landing on the north-south runway move easterly toward the terminal

Toronto International Airport

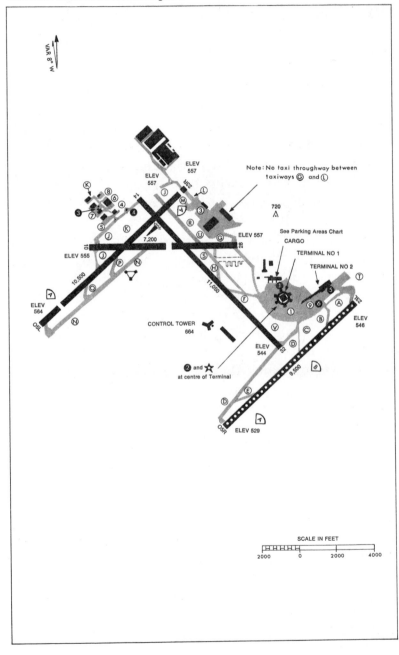

buildings. So we can expect that the first aircraft – really all of them – will head in that direction once they're on the ground."

Armstrong pointed toward the north.

"At the north end of the north-south runway we've got the Toronto Scottish dug in on each side of the runway facing south. The ground is lower there than it is at the south end of the airfield, so they'll have a good shot with their TOW and Blowpipe missiles."

He turned to face east toward the huge Terminal One structure with the eight stories of parking garage sitting on top of it.

"We've used the open parking levels of Terminal One almost like an ancient man-of-war. We've got the Queen's York Rangers and the artillery regiment with twenty-five pounders and TOW missiles and machine guns on every floor except the roof. They have a commanding view of the entire airfield. My only concern is that if they have to fire, they know exactly where the Toronto Scottish, the 48th Highlanders – I'll come to them in a minute – and the Brits are, so they don't take our own people out."

Then Armstrong turned and walked to the south window of the control tower and pointed to the west end of Runway 5 Right.

"The 48th Highlanders are at the west end of Runway 5 Right. The button of 5 Right is lower than the eastern end of the runway, so they get a good view should the Americans come in from either direction on it. Also, the 48th are equipped with the TOW missile as well as the Blowpipe. They have five Rapiers as have the Toronto Scottish up at the north end. Each Rapier has at least fifteen missiles. Each of the TOW units – and there are thirty-two of those on the airfield, the Toronto Scottish have ten, Queen's York Rangers in Terminal One have twelve, and the other ten are with the 48th – each of them has five missiles."

37

TOW Missile Projector

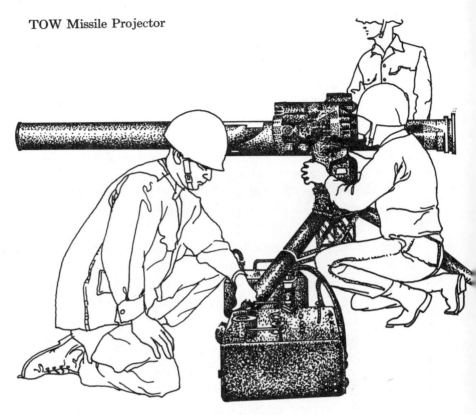

He turned back to face south again.

"Now our friends, the Brits, with their magic Rapier missiles are divided. South of the airfield at Centennial Park – that's the ski hill made out of garbage many years ago – they have twenty-one Rapiers with the Queen's Own Rifles who also have twenty Blowpipes. The Brits and the Queen's Own are on top of the hill, which gives them a superb shot at any inbound or circling aircraft. Then they have another five Rapiers with Colonel Foy and his 48th Highlanders at the west of Runway 5 Right and another five with Colonel Esplen and the Torscots to the north."

Armstrong now faced Colonel de Gaspé. "That's the deployment, sir."

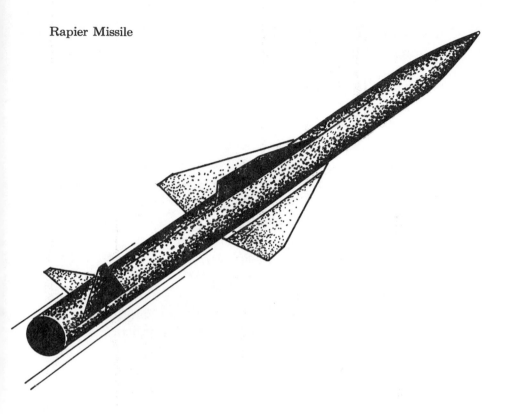

"Thank you, Colonel. Now give me your communications net again, please," de Gaspé said.

"Your command channel is number three, sir, with a backup channel number five. Only the commanding officers are on that net. They have their own channels to their own people, so there won't be any overlap."

"Good." De Gaspé looked around at his commanding officers and said, "Any questions?"

Colonel Holoduke of the Queen's York Rangers spoke up. "Sir, in the event we have to fire on one or all of the aircraft, what's the procedure? We've been briefed, but could we just go over it again, please."

Colonel de Gaspé nodded. "Okay. This is the way it goes.

If they come in on the north-south runway, the prime responsibility for aircraft on the ground will be the Toronto Scottish. You've got your TOW missiles numbered one to ten. As they land, your number one unit should pick up number one aircraft and keep trained on it. Number two should do the same with number two aircraft, and so forth, until the tenth aircraft is down. Then the Queen's York Rangers with their twelve TOW missiles numbered in sequence, should pick up the eleventh aircraft, twelfth, and so forth. The twenty-third should be picked up by the 48th and followed through. Holoduke, you're in Terminal One. You and your people have got to remember that the 48th are at the west end of Runway 5 Right. You can't fire in their direction, nor can you fire at the Toronto Scottish at the north end. Let me put it another way, if you're firing in their direction, you must do so with extreme caution.

"We will not fire at any aircraft unless the troops in it attempt to disembark contrary to my instructions. If they start to disembark, it will be my command – and my command only – upon which you are permitted to fire. The command will be, 'hit number . . . fire.' I will give you the number of the aircraft. So if it's the fourth aircraft on the ground, and it starts to disgorge people, my command will be 'hit number four, fire.' That will be your TOW missile unit number four, Esplen, which should be tracking number four airplane, and should launch on it immediately my order is passed to you."

Shepherd of the British unit asked, "And aircraft still airborne, sir?"

"Right. You will fire with your Rapier weapons only at my command. Your targets will be airborne aircraft that attempt to turn and head back for the United States. I will use the Blowpipe and Rapier in reserve. If the fighters attack us, then we'll go for them too."

De Gaspé paused, then said, "Whatever we do, gentlemen, must be done with the greatest discretion. Ideally, we will not fire at all. I'm sure that none of us has any desire whatsoever to kill or injure any of our American friends, and I have a feeling they feel the same way about us. Let's hope they do anyhow.

"One final thing. I'll be in the tower with the air traffic controllers, brave souls that they are. Colonel Armstrong will be in the backup control unit in the vehicles to the west of the tower." De Gaspé smiled at Walnek and Spence, who returned the smile rather self-consciously.

"Any further questions?" he asked as he looked around the glass-walled room. The light of the sun disappearing below the horizon in the clear sky to the west silhouetted his commanders against the terminal buildings, hangars, and runways of the vast Toronto International Airport. There were no questions.

Suddenly they were startled by the loud voice from the traffic controllers loudspeaker system. "Tower, this is radar. I'm getting a formation of unidentified aircraft at the outer limit of my range at a bearing of about one six zero. Looks to me like about thirty aircraft. They appear to be tracking on a heading of three four zero, which should put them over Rochester in five, their speed and altitude unknown at this time."

Walnek was at his microphone immediately. "Okay, radar, give me your speed on those aircraft as quickly as you can, and an estimate as to what time they might arrive here, assuming they're coming here."

The voice came back, "Will do, Tower . . . good God, I'm just picking up another gaggle. Looks to me like perhaps fifty of them strung out. They're on a bearing of about two zero five, their track also looks like Rochester!"

Walnek was calm. "Yeah. Looks like they're going to rendezvous across the lake. Have you got an ETA for me yet?"

With a slight pause, radar came back. "Looks like eighteen forty-five, about twenty minutes from now."

Colonel de Gaspé, his voice raised with excitement, shouted to his commanders, "All right, chaps, get moving."

As they rushed out, he turned to Walnek. "Get a red alert signal out immediately." Walnek nodded and reached for his telephone. De Gaspé grabbed the one next to it and quickly dialled the direct line to the Commander of Mobile Command at St. Hubert. A soft voice. "Christie here."

"Sir, it's de Gaspé in the control tower at Toronto. They're on their way. We've picked up about eighty of them. Apparently they're going to rendezvous at Rochester. Assuming they're coming here, they'll arrive about eighteen forty-five hours."

Lieutenant-General Christie did not respond for a moment, then said, "That's just about when the President will finish his television address. Keep me posted. I'm in my battle command room at this time. I'll report immediately to the Vice-Chief in Ottawa."

Ottawa
Tuesday, October 7, 1980, 6:26 P.M.

The Vice-Chief of the Defence Staff, General White, turned to the CDS in the battle operations room of the Alternate Command Centre near Ottawa and gave him Christie's report on de Gaspé's information, then asked, "What about the Prime Minister, sir."

The CDS ran his hand through his thick hair and looked up at the wall clock. Eighteen twenty-six hours. Robert Porter would just be driving through the gates of the long driveway into Government House, where he was to meet the Governor-General.

As the CDS dialled the Government House number, he glanced around the operations room at the green-uniformed Canadian Armed Forces men and women receiving reports from across Canada on the status of Operation Reception Party. They posted the incoming information on boards, maps, and charts so the CDS and his staff could monitor quickly the input which was now flowing rapidly.

When the switchboard operator came on at Government House, the CDS gave her terse instructions that the line was to be left clear for him on an emergency basis so he could communicate with the Prime Minister at will. The operator found the Governor-General's executive assistant in the front lobby of Government House waiting for the arrival of the Prime Minister. The CDS waited. Within two minutes Porter was on the line.

When he had received the CDS's report, he said, calmly, "Well, we still can't be exactly certain what their intent is. The main thing is we're ready. I'm just going to join the Governor-General. I don't propose to tell him about this until I have to. It may be a bluff, but we'll soon find out. Call me as soon as they've committed to landing."

The CDS's call back to the Prime Minister coincided with the final words of the President's invasion announcement ten minutes later at eighteen thirty-nine hours, 6:39 P.M., when, without any knowledge of the existence of the plans for Operation Reception Party, the Governor-General thought he had no choice but to follow the instructions of the President.

Toronto
Tuesday, October 7, 1980, 6:41 P.M.

De Gaspé's body tensed as he heard the first southern-accented words of the American leader through the control tower loudspeaker. "Toronto Arrival, this is USAF Blueforce leader. Over."

Toronto Arrival's voice came back instantly, as briefed. "USAF Blueforce leader, Toronto Arrival. Go."

The American leader read his message, which was as much an announcement: "Toronto Arrival, Blueforce leader. I am Major-General Dudley Smith, personally appointed by the President of the United States to lead the USAF Blueforce to land at Toronto International Airport and Downsview Canadian Forces Base for the purpose of taking over military occupancy and government of the Metropolitan Toronto area and southern Ontario in accordance with the President's decree that Canada should become and is now part of the United States of America."

Toronto Arrival broke in. "We have monitored the President's statement, sir."

"Okay, Toronto Arrival, since this is a peaceful invasion exercise, please be advised of my requirements. They are as follows: A normal straight-in approach clearance is requested for all Blueforce aircraft into Toronto International. I have sixty Hercules and Starlifters with me for Toronto International and twenty-one into Downsview. For Toronto International I request, as I said, straight-in

45

approach on Runway 32 for all my aircraft. We will be landing in close sequence. After landing, you will marshall us to
positions on the ramps of both Terminals One and Two.
You will instruct your ground-handling people to open all
doors and gates leading into both terminals. Also instruct
your ground-handling people to marshall all buses and
trucks in the airfield area and have them stand by. We have
our own vehicles on board but we will need extras. And we
have helicopters following us in with an ETA of twenty
minutes from now."

Toronto Arrival replied, "Roger, Blueforce leader. Will
you require fuel?"

"Negative," came the Blueforce leader's voice.

"Okay, Blueforce leader. Go to Toronto Tower on 118.0
now."

In the control tower, there was a silence for a few seconds. Then it came.

"Toronto Tower, this is USAF Blueforce leader, ten miles
back at five thousand feet, clear for straight-in approach on
32. I have sixty–six zero–aircraft with me, and this call is
for clearance for all to land. Over."

De Gaspé stood looking out the southern glass wall of
the control tower beside Walnek, who put his microphone
to his mouth and said, "Roger, Blueforce leader. This is
Toronto Tower. Do not have you visual yet. We have a lot
of haze this evening. Have been monitoring your discussion
with Toronto Arrival. You're cleared for a straight-in
approach on 32 with the sixty–six zero–aircraft with you.
The twenty-one aircraft bound for Downsview should go to
126.2 at this time. The wind is zero two zero at fifteen to
twenty, the altimeter is twenty-nine decimal nine two.
Over."

"Blueforce leader," the acknowledgement came back.

With those words, de Gaspé saw the first flickering of

landing lights over the lake. He turned to Walnek and pointing said excitedly, "There they are."

As he watched, the first signs of the lead aircraft were quickly followed by the emergence of another, then another, until a small section of the darkened sky over Lake Ontario appeared to be filled with the twinkling lights of fireflies.

Walnek spoke into the microphone.

"Blueforce leader, Toronto Tower. Suggest you land long and exit on the right on Runway 5 Left at the north end. What will be the landing interval between your aircraft?"

"About twenty seconds, I reckon," an answer came back. "I know you civilian controllers don't like to have but one airplane on the runway. But this is a military operation and we'd like to get all our airplanes down as fast as we can. So when I'm turning right off onto Runway 5 Left, number two and three aircraft'll be on the ground behind me, and four and five should just be ready to touch down, and so on."

"Roger, Blueforce leader. When you're on the ground, do not switch to Toronto ground control. I will maintain control of all aircraft from the tower position."

"Roger, Toronto Tower."

Then "Blueforce leader to Blueforce, I am selecting gear down, selecting gear down now!"

The voice of Toronto radar came over the loudspeaker. "Tower, I'm painting a gaggle of fast-moving aircraft coming in from the Buffalo sector. They're just crossing the smokestacks now. They're probably at low level."

De Gaspé saw Walnek's eyes shift from watching the ever brighter landing lights of the inbound transports toward the position of the four hydro electric power station smokestacks on the shore of Lake Ontario to the southwest of the airport. As de Gaspé followed his gaze, he could see about three miles away, almost at treetop level, the clustered snouts of a dozen fighter aircraft, with missiles and bombs drooping under their wings, hurtling straight at them.

"This is it," said de Gaspé as he waited, transfixed, expecting to see missiles or bombs leave the fighters. He was absolutely helpless. There was no protection at all.

But the jets were by in two seconds as the formation thundered across the airfield with no attempt to attack.

Radar was on again. "Tower, I have three more fast-moving gaggles, one from the west at about thirty miles, another from the southeast at eighteen, and the third from the southwest, also at eighteen."

"Yeah, radar," said Walnek, "fighter squadrons – they're covering the landings of the big birds. Stand by, one."

Walnek picked up his microphone, "Toronto Tower to USAF fighter squadron leader, do you read. Over."

Silence.

"Toronto Tower to USAF fighter leader. Over."

Still no response.

"Blueforce leader is clear final," came the American's call for the final clearance to land.

De Gaspé turned away from the northeast where he had been watching the fighter squadron turning in a wide arc westerly toward Bramalea, swinging around to come back across the airfield again. His eyes went back to the long line of huge transport aircraft stretching for miles behind the leader, like a flock of geese strung out and up into the distance.

Again Walnek spoke into his microphone. "Blueforce leader is clear to land. Check gear down and locked. Wind is zero two five at fifteen."

"Blueforce leader."

Walnek muttered to de Gaspé. "The lead craft is a C141

Starlifter, the one behind it is a Hercules and most of the rest appear to be Hercs."

De Gaspé moved over to the east wall of the glass control tower and picked up the microphone Walnek had assigned to him. He watched, fascinated, as the huge leading Starlifter aircraft, appearing to be barely moving at all, almost hanging in the sky, completed its flareout well down the runway, tail down, its tires smoking as they touched. A short distance behind was the second aircraft, then the third, and the rest strung out almost as far as the eye could see.

Overhead, de Gaspé caught the flash of a turning squadron of American fighter aircraft. Walnek saw him look up and said, "We now have four fighter squadrons with us. Let's hope they've been instructed not to attack. I don't know what frequency they're on yet."

De Gaspé merely nodded.

The second USAF transport aircraft had touched down. The third was about to put its wheels on the runway. Blueforce leader was reaching the end of his landing run and beginning his turnoff onto Runway 5 Left. Then he was clear and number four and number five aircraft were on the runway.

Now de Gaspé spoke into his microphone; his voice was calm, but his hand shaking. "Blueforce leader, this is the Canadian military commander at Toronto International. For communication purposes, I will be called Reception leader. Do you read?"

"Blueforce leader, go."

"Okay, Blueforce leader, this message should be copied by all of your aircraft and passed on to your fighters. Each of your aircraft on the ground is covered by a TOW missile and each of your aircraft in the air is covered by a surface-to-air missile. In addition, the entire airfield is covered by

49

light artillery and machine guns. You are to carry out the following instructions. In the event you fail or refuse to follow these orders, I will destroy your entire fleet and can do so instantly.

"Blueforce leader, you are to continue taxiing along taxiway Romeo toward Terminal One and all aircraft on the ground or airborne are to continue to land as originally planned. No aircraft commander is to permit troops or personnel to disembark and no aircraft still airborne is to attempt to make a run for the United States. Any aircraft that permits troops to disembark or, if airborne, turns for the United States, will be immediately destroyed. Do you copy, Blueforce leader."

De Gaspé's eyes were on the huge lead aircraft taxiing southeasterly toward Terminal One, followed fifty yards behind by Blueforce number two, and then by number three, which was just turning right onto Runway 5 Left. There were another four aircraft on Runway 32 at this time.

Blueforce leader's voice had evidence of shock.

"Who the hell do you think you are! This was supposed to be a peaceful landing! You haven't got all that fire power. You're bluffing, man, you're bluffing!"

De Gaspé's voice was cold and firm. "Blueforce leader, I am not bluffing."

Suddenly a new voice. "Blueforce leader, this is Blueforce two. He's goddamn well bluffing and these goddamn Canadians haven't got anything. I've got a planeful of Green Berets. I'm going to call the bluff right now!"

The number two aircraft, a Hercules, then swung sharply to the west on Taxiway Sierra where it came to an abrupt stop. The side entrance doors flew open and the tail loading ramp began to lower. De Gaspé had his command microphone in his left hand. Into it he shouted, "Hit number two—fire! Hit number two—fire!" He could hear Foy's voice feed back. "Hit number two—fire! Hit number two—fire!" De Gaspé automatically counted the seconds. "A thousand and one, a thousand and two." The ramp of the Herc was still lowering. In the gathering dusk, men were leaping out of the doors . . . "a thousand and three" . . . then in one instant the entire aircraft became a huge ball of orange-yellow flame enveloping the green, running bodies around it. In a split second, the fuselage expanded like a toy balloon, then exploded, spewing out pieces of equipment, bodies, and more fire. The force of the blast shook the control tower glass, almost shattering it.

Into the microphone in his right hand, de Gaspé said, still with a cool unbroken voice, "Reception leader to all Blueforce aircraft. I repeat, you are not to disembark any troops, and all aircraft still airborne are to land. Aircraft on the ground are to keep rolling toward the parking ramps at Terminals One and Two. Follow the 'Follow Me' vehicle in front of you, Blueforce leader. You will be marshalled by ground personnel when you get there."

The American leader did not acknowledge de Gaspé. Instead his agitated voice was heard calling, "Blueforce leader to all helicopters—turn back, turn back."

Toronto radar's voice again. "I'm tracking one aircraft about three miles south doing a 180 degree turn toward the lake."

De Gaspé rushed to the south window and tried to find the turning aircraft, but couldn't. Back to his communications microphone, he barked, "Shepherd, one of them is doing a 180 toward the lake. He should be just to the south of you."

Shepherd was back immediately. "I've got him, sir."

"Then fire! Fire!"

"Firing, sir! Firing!" Shepherd acknowledged.

Walnek protested. "Shouldn't you have given them another warning?"

51

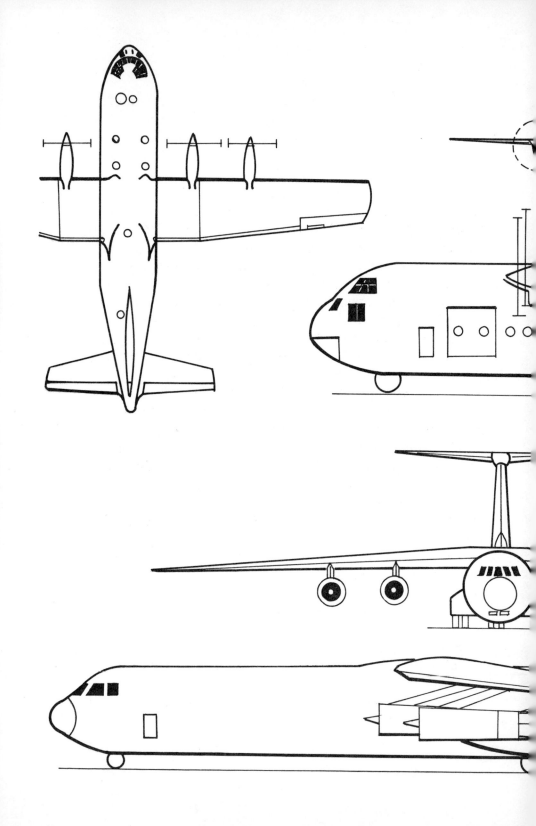

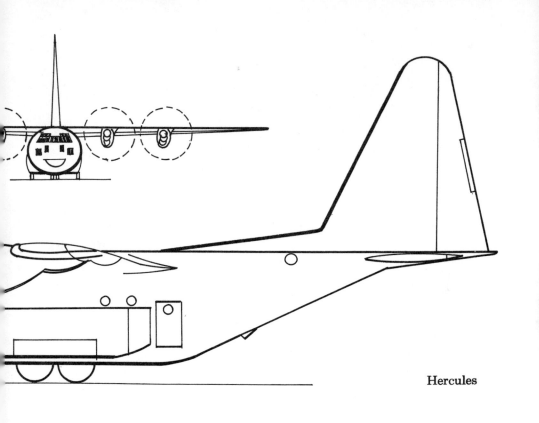

Hercules

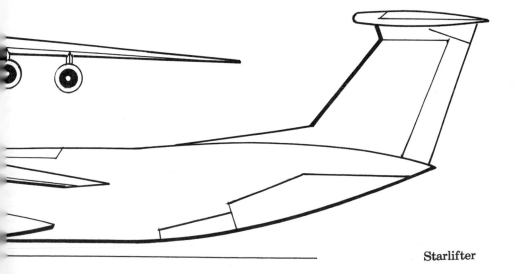

Starlifter

De Gaspé shook his head. "No way. They've had their warning. Things are moving too fast."

Again de Gaspé was back to the American leader. "Blueleader, this is Reception leader. Will you please give me the frequency your fighter squadrons are on? We've been trying to pick it up and can't."

At that instant—just as the words "They're on emergency radar frequency 121.5" came back—the darkening sky to the south of the airport lit up like instant sunlight as the massive warhead of Shepherd's Rapier missile detonated on contact with the inboard port engine of the enormous fuel-, man-, and equipment-laden Hercules. The explosives in the warhead, coupled with the thousands of gallons of jetfuel ignited by the blast, created an enormous orange meteor of flame, spreading a trail of engines, bodies, and pieces of the aircraft as it disintegrated in the centre core of the inferno.

Walnek watched with disbelief, shaking his head from side to side. But de Gaspé was concentrating on his next critical move.

"Mr. Walnek, give me 121.5 as quickly as you can."

Walnek reached out to the selector switch on his panel, turned to the 121.5 frequency and gave de Gaspé a quick thumbs-up signal.

De Gaspé looked out the control tower windows through 360 degrees, looking hard for the fighter squadrons. He said tersely to Walnek, "I'm going to talk to the fighters. While I'm doing that, ask radar to tell you where they are. I can't see them."

Then he spoke into his tower microphone. "USAF fighter squadron leaders, this is the Canadian military commander at Toronto International—Reception leader. I will not ask you to acknowledge until I am finished. All of your transport aircraft assigned to Toronto International have landed or are in the process of landing. As at this moment,

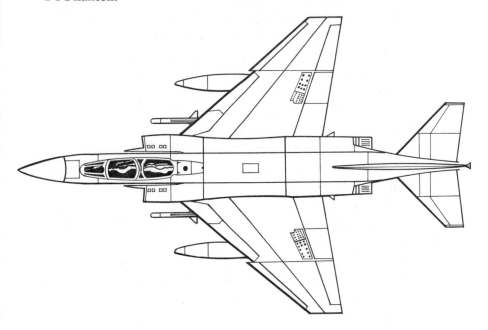

they are not yet prisoners of war and are still open to attack by my forces in the event they commit any further hostile actions contrary to my instructions.

"I have already been forced to destroy two of them. I do not know what your instructions are about strafing or bombing in support of your troops or transport aircraft, but I will tell you this . . . the moment you commence an attack on any one of my ground positions, I will immediately order my missile people to destroy you and every one of your transport aircraft, whether in the air or on the ground."

Walnek had shoved a sketch in front of him showing the location of the four fighter squadrons—about forty-eight aircraft. The diagram hastily drawn by Walnek showed that the four squadrons had apparently made a rendezvous at the Kleinberg VOR* station fifteen miles north of the

*VOR–VHF omni-directional Range.

Toronto International Airport, and the lead squadron had just left that location headed directly for the airport, with the second, third, and fourth squadrons following with two-mile intervals between them. It was obvious to de Gaspé that this formation was set up for strafing and bombing so that the first squadron could make its attack and clear before the next wave came in. Another minute and a half and the first wave would be on top of them.

Back to the microphone. "Reception leader to the lead USAF fighter squadron commander. Have you copied my message?"

The response was immediate. The voice coming through the loudspeaker was angry and venomous, "Yes, I have, you blackmailing bastard."

De Gaspé half shouted into his microphone, "My instructions to you are to break off immediately and to return to your bases. I give you ten seconds to acknowledge in the affirmative and to commence your break-off by a turn to the starboard."

De Gaspé barked into his command communications microphone in his left hand, still pressing the switch on his tower transmitter so the fighters could hear, "All missile commanders, standby, standby! There are four fighter squadrons approaching from the north at low level. If the fighter squadrons do not break off in ten seconds, I will give the order to fire on all aircraft on the ground and in the air. All Rapiers track the fighters. Standby one!"

De Gaspé's eyes went to the huge second sweeping clock in the control tower as he measured the last five seconds of the response time he had given the lead American squadron commander.

On the ninth second, it came. "Number one squadron is breaking off and returning to base. Turning starboard now."

Then a new voice. "Number two squadron following."

Then another. "Number three squadron following."

And the final. "Number four squadron following."

Radar's voice came through strong and clear. "All squadrons are turning west, turning west."

De Gaspé could see them now, very low, as the lead squadron was part way through its turn to the west. It was no more than half a mile to the north of the Toronto International Airport, just beyond Malton, the swept back wings of its twelve F4 Phantom aircraft glitteringly etched against the crimson sky and the sun just disappearing below the horizon.

De Gaspé's shoulders seemed to sag slightly as the high pressure of that moment of tension was eased.

'Reception leader to missile commanders. The fighter squadrons have broken off. Maintain watch on all aircraft on the ground and inbound."

Walnek turned to him and said, "We have thirty-eight aircraft on the ground, two destroyed, and radar informs we've got another twenty inbound."

De Gaspé looked at his watch. "Could you split them and bring half in on Runway 5 Right and the other half on Runway 5 Left? If you could do that we could speed up the landing time considerably."

Walnek checked the wind direction and speed, and replied. "Yeah. The wind is now zero three zero at about twelve, so these big birds should have no problem."

Into his microphone Walnek said, "The three USAF aircraft on final for 32 below seventeen hundred feet indicated are to continue on final for 32 and land. The remaining aircraft above seventeen hundred feet indicated will turn port downwind for landings on Runway 5 Right and Runway 5 Left. The number one aircraft will take 5 Left, the number two aircraft 5 Right, and the remaining aircraft will alternate accordingly. It is not necessary to acknowledge this transmission except if you have any questions or difficulty."

Silence followed Walnek's instructions, and de Gaspé could see the fourth aircraft in the landing line begin a slow turn to its left toward the west. The landing lights of the aircraft following it began the westward turn almost in unison.

Walnek nodded affirmatively. "They've got it."

De Gaspé paused for a moment to take a look at the incredible sight spread out in front of him. At the far eastern end of the Terminal Two ramp, he could see the flashing navigation lights of Blueforce leader's aircraft becoming brighter as darkness descended. He could still see the aircraft clearly as it was being led to its parking position by the ground control vehicle, the red signal light on its roof flashing insistently.

Strung out behind the leader in an unending line from Terminal Two westerly around the Terminal One ramp, and north along Taxiway Romeo to the exit points from the northerly end of 32, stretched the long line of the huge Starlifters and Hercules moved slowly. Their green and red navigation lights and flashing white strobes looked to de Gaspé like a string of Christmas lights as they passed by the darkened Terminal One. He wondered whether the crews on board the American transports could see the muzzles of the guns and missiles trained on them from the parking levels above the terminal.

"Reception leader to Blueforce leader."

"Blueforce leader, go," came the American General's response.

"When you have been marshalled and parked, sir, and this applies to all Blueforce aircraft, you are to remain inside your aircraft. No one, I repeat, no one, is to open a door, lower a ramp, or in any way attempt to disembark from any of your aircraft. When you have shut down, you will continue to monitor Toronto Tower for further instructions."

Blueforce leader repeated the instructions de Gaspé had given him, and then proceeded to get a copy check from all his aircraft by asking them to acknowledge by their numbers in sequence. He knew that the Canadian military commander's instructions were crucial for the safety of each aircraft and its crew and passengers, so no chance could be taken that one of the crews had missed the instructions.

While this check was going on, Colonel de Gaspé reported to the commander at Mobile Command at the operations room at St. Hubert.

General Christie was delighted. "Excellent, Pierre, excellent. We've got them at Downsview, and here at St. Hubert, and at Dorval and right across the country, but yours is the only place that had to take a shot at them. American troops and vehicles started to move across the bridges along the Great Lakes system, so we blew sections of them as planned. That stopped them right in their tracks. They didn't try to come through the tunnel at Windsor though. Guess they knew that if it was blown, it would be a real deathtrap.

"So we've stopped them for the moment in the East. Reception Party has worked right across the board. Winnipeg, Edmonton, Calgary, Vancouver, Cold Lake, everywhere. They made their landings simultaneously almost to the minute. If they had staggered their timing, then the first ones in could have warned the others across the country, but they didn't plan it that way. Strange."

De Gaspé asked, "What about their ground movements in the West, sir?"

"I haven't got a reading on that yet. They should be hitting our roadblocks starting in about twenty minutes. The air landings began twenty-four minutes ago, so it will be pretty close to an hour before they reach our people in Manitoba, Saskatchewan, and Alberta. Intelligence informs us they're on the move there, but apparently no attempt has been made to move in by land into British Columbia."

Christie broke off, "Sorry. Must go, Pierre. The CDS wants me to give him my report so he can brief the Prime Minister. Keep up the good work."

Washington
Tuesday, October 6, 1980, 7:12 P.M.

The atmosphere in the Oval Office of the White House was tense. The President, white hair dishevelled, suit-coat off, tie unloosened at the neck, sat at his desk. He was reading a report which had just been brought to him and at the same time keeping his ear tuned to the television set, listening to the news reports and commentary on his speech and the progress of the annexation of Canada.

Sitting on the edge of the couch to the right of the President's desk was Irving Wolf, his Secretary of State, the man whose advice and strategies had brought him to this moment of confrontation with the Canadians. Wolf had drafted the original ultimatum and had convinced the reluctant President of its value. Wolf sat now, head down, gaze on the floor, his nose between his two index fingers, as he listened to the television announcer.

Pacing back and forth, but out of the President's and Wolf's line of sight, was the Secretary of Defence, J. William Crisp, a round man of medium height and age. Crisp had been a naval hero during the Korean War, and had caught the President's eye many years ago. The financial support he had provided had greatly helped the President during his campaign.

As an industrialist from the Midwest, Crisp knew nothing at all about Canada, except that it lay to the north of the United States and had a lot of oil and natural gas – gas that was desperately needed by the United States. Mostly it was American money that had discovered it. The country, so far as he knew, was still run by England and the Queen. It had no defence force except a Regular Force of 50,000, of which maybe 5,000 at the outside might be combat trained, and a nondescript Reserve Force of about 30,000, most of whom were militia troops, with about 1,200 Air Reservists made up of eight squadrons, flying—and Crisp wouldn't believe it when he was briefed—single-engine Otters, an antique light transport aircraft produced in Canada in the 1950's, and a handful of Second World War DC3s.

When Crisp had received the recommendation of the Joint Chiefs of Staff for Operation Northland, he was forced by his own ignorance of Canada to rely totally on the battle plan they submitted. Unfortunately for Crisp, while the Joint Chiefs of Staff and their immediate staff had the military and logistic statistics on Canada, their general attitude toward Canada and their knowledge of the country, its people, its government, and its background were similar to those of Crisp himself.

Operation Northland had been based on the thesis that the Canadians had no real defence force and that, in any event, Canada would welcome the Americans and capitulate immediately without a fight.

Since the President was right in the middle of a heavy campaign for re-election, he was also concerned about the reaction of American multi-national corporations to any destruction of their Canadian investments. This factor weighed heavily on Crisp's thinking when he approved the walk-ride-fly-in approach submitted by the Joint Chiefs of Staff, and rejected their proposal for an all-out paratroop and "Heliborne" assault for openers.

So, if Operation Northland failed, J. William Crisp, as Secretary of Defence, would be the first one to carry the can and be fired, but it would be the President, the Commander-in-Chief of all United States forces, who would take the responsibility.

By 7:12, the three men in the Oval Office of the White House knew they had failed, that the Canadians had been totally misjudged, and that all 228 Starlifters and Hercules and the over 15,000 men on board this great air armada were at this moment trapped in their aircraft on airfields all across Canada.

News of their capture had not yet reached the media and had not come across in the television bulletins, but the President and the two men in the room with him knew, and they knew it was total disaster for them.

The conversations between the military commanders at all Canadian commercial and military bases and the air commander assigned to each had been fully monitored by the U.S. Federal Aeronautics Authority and military controllers. The sequence of the landing actions had been reported by the commanders of the covering fighter squadrons. All of them had been ordered not to strafe, bomb, or use their missiles except in the event of Canadian attack on the transport aircraft, which was the situation at Toronto.

Using these monitored reports, the chairman of the Joint Chiefs of Staff (JCS) had kept the President informed on open line from the Pentagon. A final call from the JCS Chairman confirmed the worst. All aircraft and airtroops had been captured. Only the following helicopters had been able to turn back before they came into missile range. The bridges on the Great Lakes system had been blown. The only possible hope was that the tank and armoured car columns which had crossed the western U.S./Canadian border east of the Rockies might achieve their objectives and take the major Canadian cities there.

As he listened to the chairman of the JCS certifying the Canadian coup, the President shook his head in disbelief.

"General, how in God's name could you have misread the situation so badly?" With that he transfixed Crisp with a look that stopped him right in his tracks. "Do you realize we'll be the laughing stock of the world? Now listen to this one carefully, General. I want the answer in ten minutes, and it had better be good. The question is simple. What do we do next?" He slammed on the phone, and looked again at Crisp.

The President shouted a fast resumé of the disastrous news from the chairman of the Joint Chiefs of Staff. His voice rising, he shouted even louder.

"For Christ sake, how could you people have been so stupid? Sure, the Canadians have a small force. It's next to nothing. Sure, our forefathers all got off the same boat. Sure, we speak the same language, and sure, the United States owns most of the country. But those people have a fighting record in the First World War and the Second World War like you wouldn't believe. Crisp, why the hell didn't you have our fighters clean out the airfields with bombs and rockets before transports went in? And what happened to our intelligence people? Didn't they report any troop movements? And how in God's name did we fail to track the RAF transport aircraft bringing the commandos and paratroopers across? Your people in the Pentagon are stupid beyond belief!"

The President turned in his chair and stabbed his left hand toward a map of Canada that had been hastily draped over a briefing board brought into the office. "And what about our troops moving across the border into the Canadian West?" he shouted, "I know what's going to happen to them and I know what's going to happen to us. The Canadians are going to stop us cold. Not by troops, not by weapons, but by the Prime Minister calling me on that goddamn phone, that red phone right there. Look at it! He's going to call me, and he's going to say, if your tanks, armoured vehicles, personnel carriers, anything—if they go beyond point X, you can kiss your troops sitting in their metal capsules at airports all across Canada GOODBYE!" The President pounded the desk with his fist in total anger.

Suddenly the red telephone rang. It rang again.

The President stood up, looking at it incredulously, then slowly picked it up.

Washington
Tuesday, October 7, 1980, 7:15 P.M.

The President put the phone to his ear—it was only the second time he had used it in almost four years.

"Hello."

"Mr. President," said a female voice. The President thought he caught a slight Slavic accent.

"Yes."

"The Chairman of the Supreme Soviet wishes to speak with you, Mr. President, and I will interpret for him. Would you speak with him, Mr. President?"

"Of course, put him on."

The President clapped his hand over the telephone mouthpiece and said to Wolf and Crisp with a lift of his eyebrows, "It's Yaroslav."

The saying of Yaroslov's name brought a quick vision to the President's mind. When the two leaders had met a year earlier during the President's only visit to the Soviet Union, he had been mightily impressed by this clever man who was from the same region as Stalin. Only in his early fifties, he was highly educated and totally dedicated to Communism and the cause of the Soviet Union. Yet his knowledge about world affairs was really better than the President's. The President well remembered his easy smile, and icy blue eyes which pierced as well as perceived.

As the Chairman of the Supreme Soviet began to speak, the translation immediately and disconcertingly overrode his voice. It would be the same when the President replied.

66

There was a brief exchange of pleasantries during which the Chairman pointed out that the President's activities had caused him to be wakened at 2:00 A.M. in Moscow time, that it was now 4:15 A.M. there, and that the Chairman was still in his night clothes. The President chuckled. "Sorry about that," he said.

Then the Chairman went straight to the purpose of his unusual telephone call.

"For the past two days, the Soviet Union has been closely monitoring the position you have taken against Canada, Mr. President. We understand the position in which the United States finds itself and we can understand very well the reasons why you decided to give Canada an ultimatum, an ultimatum that could have been enforced by economic sanctions which would have brought Canada to her knees very quickly.

"Instead, you have moved to take over Canada by force, and to annex it to the United States. Unfortunately, Mr. President, this is a course of action which the Soviet Union finds totally unacceptable. Under no circumstances can we tolerate the sovereign presence of the United States in the Canadian Arctic Islands. To have your military installations in Alaska is bad enough, but to find you in a strategic position from which you can hit easily at the vital parts of the Soviet Union across the polar icecap from Ellesmere or the other Arctic Islands by aircraft or by ballistic missiles, this represents a power shift and a threat to the security of the Soviet Union which, as I have said, Mr. President, we find totally unacceptable."

The President broke in. "Mr. Chairman, we have no intention whatsoever of using the Canadian Arctic Islands for military purposes. All we want is the gas."

"That may be your intention at this instant, Mr. President, but your intentions can change at any time—to say nothing of the intentions of your successor, whoever he may be and whenever that event might occur." This last shaft was designed to let the President know the Chairman was aware of his precarious re-election position.

"To occupy Canada militarily for a short period of time is one thing, but to annex Canada and to make it part of the United States is quite another. No, Mr. President, your action against Canada is one the Soviet Union cannot live with, even though my intelligence people inform me that the Canadians, by ingenious planning and by out-thinking your military people, have led your flies into a net of spider's webs.

"I would guess that at this very moment you and your advisors are grappling with the elusive problem of what you should do next. I am sure the Canadian Prime Minister will have a suggestion or two for you in that regard, and that you will hear from him very soon, if you have not already done so. But the Soviet Union has a suggestion for you, Mr. President, and I put it forward in the strongest possible terms. On behalf of the Soviet Union, I suggest that you forthwith agree to stop the movement of your ground troops and to remove your military aircraft from Canada. I ask that I might have your response to this suggestion within the next fifteen minutes, Mr. President. I know you will wish to consult with your advisors and the time I have given you is short, but you have put me in an untenable position. Your ultimatum to the Canadians and your action to enforce their refusal to comply has left me with no choice but to give *you* an ultimatum.

"To demonstrate that the Soviet Union is serious about this course of action, Soviet submarines from the best and largest fleet in the world, equipped with long-range nuclear warhead rockets, are at this time surfacing just beyond the twelve-mile limit offshore from every major American city on both the eastern and western seaboards, and there are others with them which will not surface.

"This is a confrontation, Mr. President, but it is not of our making. We did not expect that the United States would take a military action against Canada, but nevertheless, like the Canadians, we planned for that eventuality. Therefore, our submarines are in position."

The Chairman paused, waiting for a response from the President. It came. "I don't believe you'd start a nuclear war over this, Mr. Chairman. I think you're bluffing."

"I can assure you, Mr. President, that I, like the Canadians, am not bluffing. And also, please carefully note that I have not yet said that my submarines *will* attack, nor have I threatened you with war. What I have demonstrated to you is that the Soviet Union is totally ready for this crisis. Not only is the United States not ready, but you have suffered a humiliating defeat and loss of face at the hands of the Canadians. As I have said, I wish to have the courtesy of a response to my suggestion of withdrawal within fifteen minutes. May I have your assurance that I will hear from you in that time?"

The President responded reluctantly. "You'll hear from me," he said.

As he hung up the President looked at Crisp and rasped, "Go tell the Pentagon to halt our troops in western Canada immediately. If they have engaged the Canadians, have them disengage. They are to withdraw to the United States as quickly as possible."

Irving Wolf interjected. "Surely you're not going to capitulate so quickly. We can do a massive para-drop and really go into Canada with full air support this time . . ."

"That's the way we should have done it in the first place," the President retorted, "and now we've got the Soviet Union on our backs. No, Irving, I've made up my

69

mind. We have no choice but to pull out. I'm going to salvage those men and planes sitting on Canadian airfields."

The hot line telephone rang again. Reaching for it, the President muttered, "It's got to be Porter this time." It was.

There were no pleasantries or formalities.

"Mr. President, Porter here. I now have all your transport aircraft and your airborne troops. I regard them as hostages, not prisoners of war. If you mount a further attack on us, I will have no choice but to destroy them where they sit. I can assure you that's the last thing I want to do, but if I have to, I will.

"If you agree to stop and withdraw your ground troops in western Canada and not to mount a further attack, then on those conditions I am prepared to negotiate with you for the natural gas you need. I can do that under the mandate of the resolution the House of Commons passed this afternoon."

The President asked, "And if I agree not to attack again, what then?"

"If you are prepared to negotiate, and not to attack again, then I propose a meeting on neutral ground, commencing next Monday. The neutral ground will be the French islands of St-Pierre et Miquelon in the Gulf of St. Lawrence, which will be handy for both of us – that is, if the French government will agree to play host and I believe they will."

The President, who had been standing from the beginning of his conversation with the Chairman of the Soviet Union, sat down heavily on his swivel chair, leaned back, and looked up at the ceiling, not seeing it.

"Okay, so if I agree not to mount a further attack, and agree to immediately stop and withdraw my ground troops in the West, and if I agree to negotiate, what about my men and aircraft on your airports – your hostages as you call them?"

"Simple," the Prime Minister replied. "If you agree to these conditions—and I am prepared to accept your word for it now—then immediately I am advised by my Chief of the Defence Staff that all of your ground troops have crossed back into the United States, I will release your transport aircraft and your men with them."

The President leaned forward in his chair. His Texas drawl became pronounced and his voice relaxed slightly. "Well, Prime Minister, we Texans sure know an ace when we see one. And you've got it. In fact, so far as I can see, you're holding all the cards. Okay, I'll agree to negotiate on the terms and conditions you've stated."

Robert Porter was delighted, and his voice showed it. "Good. I'll get in touch with the President of France immediately, and my External Affairs Minister will be in touch with Mr. Wolf to work out details for the St-Pierre et Miquelon meeting.

"And by the way, the Chairman of the Soviet Union called to confirm what was going on and to tell me he was going to have a word with you about sovereignty, security, and submarines. It sounds as though you got his message. When you call him in the next few minutes, Mr. President, please tell him how much I appreciate his intervention."

The President slammed down the receiver.

Ottawa
Tuesday, October 7, 1980, 10:09 P.M.

The Prime Minister was in his office in the East Block of the Parliament Buildings. The military had tried to persuade him and his government to take up quarters and administration in the war emergency underground building, but Porter had emphatically declined. Events had moved far too rapidly from the first sign of American military action for him to be any other place than in his East Block office, next to his red hot line telephone and his direct line from the Chief of Defence Staff. The same facilities existed in the emergency war building, but the Prime Minister would have no part of it. The military were operating from that location. That was good enough for him.

It was 10:09 and he was alone in his office stretched out on the sofa where he had been for about half an hour. He had suddenly felt extremely fatigued and decided that he should put his head down for a few minutes. He had asked his close friend, Senator John Thomas, and his Defence Minister if they wouldn't mind setting up shop in the outside office where they could take all incoming calls for him, with the exception of calls on the hot line or from the CDS. He had turned out the lights in the office except for a small lamp on his desk. A pillow and blanket had been produced by his secretary. He was asleep as soon as his head hit the pillow. He hadn't moved.

The first ring of the telephone brought him up to his feet

and striding quickly toward his desk. It was the direct line from the Chief of the Defence Staff. Adamson launched right in. "Sir, the last of the United States ground forces in the West have crossed back over the border as of this moment."

The Prime Minister had still been a bit groggy during the CDS's first words, but now his mind was totally alert. "Excellent, General, excellent!" he exclaimed. "Now I authorize you to release all the American transport aircraft to return direct to their home bases . . . and General I'll have more to say about this later on, but I can't tell you how grateful I am to you and your team for pulling off this incredible miracle. It's nothing short of fantastic."

Adamson's response was a quiet "Thank you, sir."

The Prime Minister went on. "Now, one final thing. I've got to get in touch with Pierre de Gaspé. I need him at the St-Pierre et Miquelon negotiations. When I started to gather my negotiating team for that one earlier this evening, I discovered that de Gaspé, as well as being the president of Petro-Canada, is also your Toronto District commander and is running Operation Reception Party at the Toronto International Airport."

The CDS responded, "He's an exceptional man, Prime Minister, there's no question about that. I'll find out where he is at this moment. He's somewhere at Toronto International and is in touch with the commander at Mobile Command at all times. Somebody from my staff will get back to you shortly."

Toronto International
Tuesday, October 7, 1980, 10:09 P.M.

De Gaspé left the control tower for a quick tour of the hulking United States airfleet strung out along the entire outside perimeter of the parking ramps of both Terminals One and Two. The monster craft were outlined vaguely by the distant floodlights from the terminal buildings. Their service engines whined away providing electrical and other control facilities in each aircraft and enabling radio contact to be maintained at all times. Lights were on in the fuselage and as well in the flight deck of each aircraft, but all navigation and landing lights had been extinguished.

As he drove up to the aircraft of Blueforce leader, de Gaspé could not overcome the urge to stop, see, and exchange words with the American General. He pulled his VHF radio-equipped Ministry of Transport car up in front of the leader's aircraft, stopped, and got out, with the car's radio microphone in his hand. He was on tower frequency. Looking up – he guessed probably about three stories in height – to the lighted cockpit where he could see the sitting, waiting figures of men. De Gaspé spoke into the microphone.

"Blueforce leader, this is Reception leader. Do you read? Over."

He could see movement from the captain's seat.

"Blueforce leader, go."

"Good evening, General Smith. I've just done a tour of

74

the airfield to visit my commanders and thought I should come by and pay my respects while we wait for our governments to make up their minds about what they're going to do next."

A startled de Gaspé was instantly bathed in a blinding white light which took him a few seconds to adjust to. The General opened his side cockpit window and stuck his head out. Against the strong landing lights de Gaspé couldn't see him all that well, but well enough.

The crew-cut American General looked grim as he said through his radio transmitter in his now unprofessional southern accent, "Ah didn't know you Canadians had that much gumption, but ah sure know it now."

Even though he was the victor, the responsibility for the death of two hundred of the General's men weighed heavily on de Gaspé. "Perhaps when this skit's finished," he said, "and you're all safe and sound back in your big bird's nest—maybe we can have a drink together sometime and figure out what *really* happened tonight."

The General's reply was blocked out by an urgent transmission from Walnek in the tower.

"Reception leader, General Christie is standing by waiting for your return call. He would not give me the message but says it is most urgent, most urgent. Over."

"I'll be there in five," de Gaspé responded crisply.

With a wave to the American General, de Gaspé climbed back into the car and was off at high speed, lights flashing, bound for the control tower on the far side of the airport.

As he bounded into the control room, Walnek handed him the telephone, "General Christie's on the line."

De Gaspé was slightly short of breath from the climb up the stairs and paused briefly before he said, "Yes, sir."

"Pierre, the Americans have completed their end of the deal and have pulled out their people in the West. The

75

Prime Minister has authorized the immediate release of all USAF transport aircraft, their crews, and passengers."

De Gaspé beamed into the telephone. "That's fantastic. I'll inform my captive southern General, Blueforce leader, and turn him loose right away."

"Right. A signal has gone out to all our other commanders across the country so all the Americans will be heading out at the same time. I wanted to call you personally Pierre, because you're the only commander who was forced into taking a shot at them. I wanted to give you the word myself, and also to let you know how pleased I am with the way you handled things. It took a lot of guts, and believe me, the unanimous opinion around here is that you've got them."

Christie did not give him a chance to respond.

"One final thing, the P.M. was astonished to find that a) you're in the Reserves, and b) that you're the military commander at Toronto International. He thinks you're supposed to be riding an oil or gas pipe somewhere as president of PetroCan. I think it was an awful shock for him when he found out where you were and what you were doing. Evidently he wants you on an emergency basis to talk about the arrangements for the meeting with the U.S. President and his staff at St-Pierre et Miquelon."

"Yes, I heard about that part of the deal."

Christie closed off. "He'll be calling you about ten-thirty. Keep the line clear. Again, great work, Pierre!"

De Gaspé hung up and immediately reached for the VHF microphone.

"Blueforce leader, this is Reception leader. Over."

"Blueforce leader, go."

"I have some news, Blueforce leader. The Prime Minister has just authorized the release of your aircraft and passengers. My instructions are that you are to be airborne as quickly as possible and you are to return directly, repeat, directly, to your bases or to the original point of pickup of your passengers or cargo."

The pleasant southern voice came back immediately, "Roger, Wilco, Reception leader."

A further caution from de Gaspé. "And my troops will maintain their alert and weapons coverage of you until you are airborne and out of range."

"Roger." A pause. "Blueforce leader to all Blueforce aircraft. Start engines, start engines – go. I will call for a start-up check in five. Out."

It was Walnek's turn. "Toronto Tower to all Blueforce aircraft, after your start-up is completed and you have been checked in with your leader, stand by, stand by for taxi instructions. Do not acknowledge at this time."

As the start-up procedures began, the twinkling, flashing green and red navigation lights came on once again. The pulsating strobe lights and red beacons atop all aircraft appeared, flashing their special signal that each aircraft was coming alive. Then as the huge engines of the aircraft started up, de Gaspé could see one, then another, then another of the angry yellow-bluish-green exhaust flames emerging from the jet exhausts then disappearing to a quiet bluish light as the engines settled down to an idle burn. And as the engines started up, the initial whine turned into a vibrating, thunderlike noise.

"Blueforce leader to Blueforce, check in, check in. Go."

De Gaspé and Walnek could hear the aircraft check in in sequence. They all reported start-up.

When the last one had called, Walnek was ready.

"Toronto Tower to all Blueforce aircraft. All aircraft parked to the east of the easterly edge of Terminal One will use Runway 23 Left for take-off. All aircraft to the west of that line will use Runway 32. Proceed to taxi in your own sequence and take off at your own intervals when ready. After take-off, maintain visual watch for other aircraft – there are too many of you for Toronto departure or radar to handle. Normal ATC* clearance is waived. On take-off go to Rochester Approach Control, on 119.55. I will repeat, I will repeat, because I cannot ask acknowledgements from you."

With that, Walnek repeated his entire message, at the end of which the southern voice returned.

"Toronto Tower, this is Blueforce leader, we copy your instructions which are . . ." And he then repeated them, giving Walnek confirmation that the leader had it right and giving the aircraft commanders a third opportunity to hear.

"Blueforce leader moving out now, moving out now."

Slowly and deliberately, the mass of air machinery – dull, almost invisible objects in the darkness but illuminated partly by their own lights – began to move in two solemn processions along the ramps and the taxiways toward the runways assigned to them.

Another instruction from the General: "Blueforce leader to all Blueforce aircraft. Once airborne, you will proceed independently to the point of original pickup of your passengers or load."

As the General's aircraft approached the button of Runway 23 Left on Taxiway Alpha, Walnek transmitted to him.

"Toronto Tower to Blueforce leader, you're cleared for take-off. The wind is slightly on your tail at zero two five at fifteen. You're cleared for a left turn out on course. The lead aircraft on Taxiway Delta for Runway 32, you also are cleared for take-off and for left turn out on course. All aircraft following in sequence are clear to go without any further clearance from this tower."

*ATC – Air Traffic Control.

Through the clear windows of the control tower, completely dark except for the dim blue illuminating lights, de Gaspé could hear and feel the thunder of the massive jet engines as they went to full thrust and power. Blueforce leader's troop-loaded Starlifter moved ever faster down the runway to its rotation speed, then lifted off the ground smoothly, gracefully, just opposite the button of Runway 32, where Blueforce 28 was swinging onto the runway, landing lights switched on, then rolling for take-off.

For the next twelve minutes, the clear night air for miles around the Toronto International Airport was filled with the continuous vibrating roar from the huge jet engines of the Starlifters and the screaming turboprop power plants of the Hercules as they rushed like a flock of frightened big birds to escape from a place of sudden danger.

As the last aircraft was rotating on liftoff from Runway 32, Walnek answered the telephone, then handed it without a word to de Gaspé.

His eyes still following the lights of the climbing machines, he said, "De Gaspé here."

It was a familiar voice. "Pierre, it's Tom Scott. The P.M. wants to have a word with you. Hang on."

In a moment Robert Porter came on. His voice was that of a happy, confident man.

He opened good naturedly. "Pierre, for God's sake, how many hats do you wear? I go looking for the president of Petro-Canada to tell him I need him immediately to start organizing the meeting with the President, and where do I find him? He's my military commander at Toronto and the key man in the success of Operation Reception Party!

"Even though I've known you for years, Pierre, I had no idea you were involved in the military, but I can tell you that tonight I'm delighted you are. You know, if it hadn't been for the Reserves, we would never have done it."

"May be, sir," de Gaspé replied. "But on the other hand, let's face it, it's the Regular Force, small in number as they are, who've kept it all together since Korea. We've worked Reception Party as a team with them and with the Brits."

"True, true," the Prime Minister agreed, then changed his tone. "I want to talk with you about the meeting at St-Pierre et Miquelon, Pierre, but before we get into that, what's going on at Toronto International? Are there still American aircraft on the ground there?"

"No, sir. The last one was airborne just as you called. I can still see him." As he talked, de Gaspé turned to look out the control room windows to the north, then to the west and south. "I can still see him and the nav lights of – I guess maybe twenty of his buddies, all hightailing it in different directions back south of the border."

The Prime Minister's voice sounded subdued for a moment. "I still can't believe they attacked us. It's just incredible. What's even more incredible – in fact, it's just ridiculous – is that this sort of thing could happen at all. The Americans have taken us for granted for so long – their Presidents never come here, their Secretaries of State rarely come here. They really don't know anything about Canada. It's a goddamn shame. However, they did it. The thing I really regret is that you had to destroy those two aircraft."

De Gaspé was on the defensive immediately. "I had no choice, sir."

"Pierre, I know that. I wasn't being critical. I was just saying that I regret it had to be done. I agree with you. You had absolutely no choice whatsoever. Were there any survivors?"

"None, not even from the one on the ground. We'll start the cleanup operation right away."

They had arrived at the reason for the Prime Minister's call.

"Well, I'm afraid you're going to have to leave that for somebody else to handle, Pierre, because I want you up here in Ottawa right away. We've got only four days to get ready for the St-Pierre et Miquelon meeting with the President. When we meet with that bastard, we've got to be prepared.

"I want you here in my East Block office at eight o'clock in the morning. I've instructed the Chief of the Defence Staff to release you from your command. There'll be a Jet Star in at Downsview at six in the morning to pick you up."

In the now quiet darkness of the control tower, de Gaspé could see the lights of vehicles converging on the area of the blown-up transport aircraft, but his mind was still totally on the conversation with his Prime Minister.

"I'll be there, sir."

"And Pierre, I've got one final thing to say to you. It may sound somewhat un-Canadian."

De Gaspé was startled. "What's that, sir?"

"I'm goddamn proud of you."

Hôtel Île-de-France, St-Pierre et Miquelon
Tuesday, October 14, 1980, 10:00 A.M.

It took a lot to get Pierre de Gaspé nervous. At this moment, he was.

The Prime Minister had asked de Gaspé to backstop him in presenting Canada's position on the various transportation modes which would have to be considered before deciding which one or which combination would carry the urgently needed natural gas from the Canadian Arctic Islands to the energy-short American market.

Part of his mind recorded the sight as he looked around the vast new dining chamber of the Hôtel Île-de-France now being used as the conference room for this historic confrontation, while the other part of his mind worked over the facts, figures, and approach he and his assistants had prepared and the Prime Minister had approved.

The huge chamber was of typical Norman-French design, solid stone and mortar laced with wooden beams against a high white ceiling, elaborately carved heavy doors, and a highly polished wooden floor. At the end of the room, at de Gaspé's left, just behind the seat of the chairman at the head of the U-formed conference table, an elegant, superbly carved stone fireplace dancing with flame threw its welcome into the chilled room, a place which would become much warmer as the negotiations progressed.

The chairman had not yet entered the room, but three of his staff of four were already seated at their places on each side of his chair. Nor had the Prime Minister of Canada or the President of the United States arrived.

The seat to de Gaspé's immediate right was empty, waiting for the Prime Minister. The remainder of the chairs on the Canadian side were filled by the Minister of Energy, Mines and Resources on the Prime Minister's immediate right, then the Minister of External Affairs. On de Gaspé's left was the chairman of the National Energy Board, Kenneth Atrill, who had been appointed by the Prime Minister only six weeks before. His background as Deputy Minister of Energy in Alberta had failed to prepare him for the major burden of carrying out the preparation and conduct of these most difficult negotiations with the Americans. The Prime Minister had seen that his most reliable advice would have to come from Pierre de Gaspé, and that the new NEB chairman would not resent that confidence.

De Gaspé made an observation to Atrill, "Thank God there are no press permitted at this meeting." He got an agreeing nod from Atrill, then looked across to the men seated at the opposite wing of the conference table.

To right of the still-vacant chair of the President sat Irving Wolf, elbows on the table, nose between the index fingers. On Wolf's right, the heavy-jowled, rotund head of the U.S. Federal Power Commission, a man who had said absolutely nothing on the first day of the conference but had chosen to scribble notes and pass them through the Secretary of State to the President—if Wolf thought they were worthy of passing.

On the left of the President's place was his energy czar and then the Secretary of the Interior.

Sitting to the immediate rear of each of the negotiating teams were their staff people, ready to provide their masters with instant statistics, information, charts, maps, photo-

St-Pierre et Miquelon

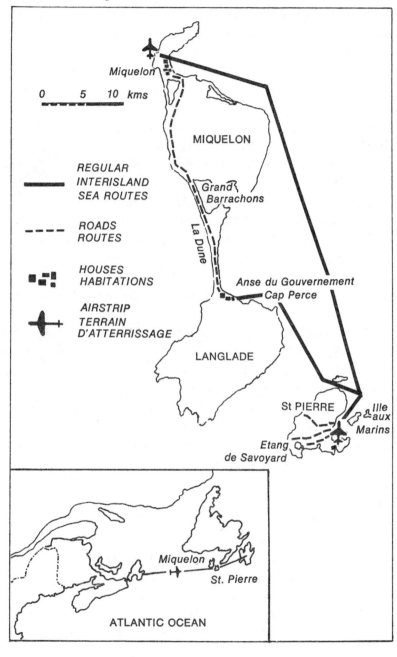

0   5   10 kms

REGULAR
INTERISLAND
SEA ROUTES

ROADS
ROUTES

HOUSES
HABITATIONS

AIRSTRIP
TERRAIN
D'ATTERRISSAGE

Miquelon

MIQUELON

Grand
Barrachons

La Dune

Anse du Gouvernement
Cap Perce

LANGLADE

St PIERRE

Ille
aux
Marins

Etang
de Savoyard

Miquelon

St. Pierre

ATLANTIC OCEAN

graphs, and sometimes their opinions–whether they were asked or not.

It was cold in the dining chamber of the Hôtel Île-de-France on October 14, 1980, the second day of this crucial conference. The question for the day was the building, location, and financing of a transportation system to carry natural gas to the United States from the Canadian Arctic Islands.

The proceedings of the first day had been chaired by the Foreign Minister of France. During that opening session, both the Canadian and United States leaders had been cool and almost hostile toward each other, but during the give and take of debate a new, well-founded regard for each other's ability had developed.

The first subject matter of the negotiations had been resolved by the end of the opening day. The United States would have access to 50 per cent of the natural gas discoveries in the Canadian Arctic Islands at a wellhead price of slightly under $1.00 U.S. per a thousand cubic feet. This was an effective Canadian price of $.89 C. because by the fall of 1980 the Canadian dollar had risen 11 per cent in value above the U.S. dollar.

Suddenly the talking among the waiting conference participants abruptly ceased as all eyes turned toward the double-doored entrance to the room. Immediately there was the sound of scraping chairs as to a man they stood as three men entered the chamber together. As he ushered them forward toward the conference table, the man in the centre held with his left hand the arm of the President of the United States, and with his right hand the arm of the Prime Minister of Canada. To the surprise of Pierre de Gaspé and all except the French participants, the man in the centre was not the Foreign Minister of France, but the enormously successful President of France, who was just finishing his

85

first term of seven years and who soon would begin his campaign for re-election.

The President of France, Valéry Giscard d'Estaing, tall, elegant, and still young at fifty-five, released his two colleagues as they approached the conference table. Each went to his designated seat and sat down. The second day of the conference got under way. The French Foreign Minister, who had followed the three into the room, took the chair immediately on the right of his President.

When everyone in the room had settled down, the President of France began.

"Monsieur le Président, Monsieur le Premier Ministre, there is no doubt that I have caught both of you off guard by arriving just a half hour ago without notice. As I have already explained to you and will now say to all members of the conference so they will understand, I thought it my high personal duty and responsibility to each of your magnificent countries, Canada and the United States, and to their people with whom the people of France have historically had the closest of connections and good relationships, both in peace and in war, in times of plenty and in times of adversity, that I should attend."

In his deliberate and forceful way, President Giscard d'Estaing alternated his gaze from the Prime Minister to the President as he spoke.

"Much of France dwells in Canada, not only in la belle province de Québec, but throughout the rest of the nation as well, where there are now some seven million French-Canadians of descent from stock which came from Normandy, Brittany, and the Basque country at the very time that these islands, St-Pierre et Miquelon, were first inhabited in the days of Jacques Cartier. That these two small islands are a part of France and not a part of Canada is almost a miracle and is a source of joy to all of France."

Then a wry smile. "On the other hand, the fact that these two islands exist in this location and are part of France within the North American complex will come as a matter of complete and total surprise to the close to 250 million people who populate your two magnificent countries." Knowing smiles from all in the chamber greeted that remark.

"Gentlemen, the nature of the dispute between your two nations, the military methods that have been used, the ramifications of those actions, and the results of this conference are of enormous importance to the Western world and its stability, both political and economic. They are of such consequence that I personally deem it of the highest order of importance that the matters between you be amicably resolved. This is why I immediately agreed with your request, Mr. Prime Minister, that this conference might be held on these islands, on neutral ground, even though the notice could scarcely have been shorter. It is for the same reason that I have put aside all other business of state and have come here to participate in this the second day of this meeting."

The long solemn face of President Valéry Giscard d'Estaing broke into a smile as he said, "Well now, gentlemen . . ." Out and on came his glasses as he picked up the sheet of paper in front of him.

He proceeded.

"The prime matter for discussion today is the transportation mode for the movement of the natural gas from the Canadian Arctic Islands to the United States market between the Boston/New York sector of the eastern seaboard and the Detroit/Chicago sector of the Midwest."

The white-haired President from Texas turned to have a brief whispered conversation with Irving Wolf on his right, then, looking at President Giscard d'Estaing, said, "Monsieur le Président, I would like to speak to this matter and outline the position of the United States if I may?"

The President of France looked to the Prime Minister, who nodded his head in assent.

"Please go ahead, Mr. President," said d'Estaing.

The President did not read but referred to his notes as he went on.

"What we're talking about here is the movement of natural gas in large quantities over a straight-line distance between 2,500 and 3,000 miles, over some of the worst terrain, most difficult climate conditions, and most prohibitive water and ice crossings to be encountered on the face of this earth. The need of the United States for this precious commodity is beyond question. The shortage of it even at this point in time has been of disastrous consequences for my country, so bad that they were able to move me and my administration toward an attempted annexation of Canada, an action which has brought us to this table. I might say Monsieur le Président, that it was an action I did not want to take against our good friends, the Canadians, but under the circumstances I felt, as President of the United States, that I had no choice. My attitude is reflected in the fact that our military action against Canada was probably one of the least warlike demonstrations of an invasion ever recorded in the books of history!"

The Prime Minister sat back and smiled.

The President was obviously ill at ease. "The United States must have that natural gas as quickly as we can get our hands on it. On the other hand, we must balance the time requirements against the cost of delivery. If we build a pipeline system—and as you know, Monsieur le Président, I've just been up to the Arctic Islands and I have seen a new method of laying large natural gas pipelines in the water under the thick ice that exists there—then it's going

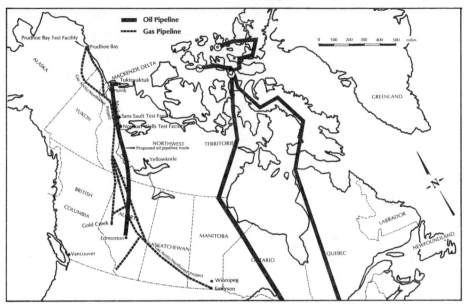

to take us another three years to lay pipe. It will have to go
from the principal source of supply, Melville Island, east to
Cornwallis Island, and then south through Somerset Island
and the Boothia Peninsula, and either down the west coast
of Hudson Bay through Manitoba and Ontario into the
United States, or, in the alternative, east from the Boothia
Peninsula, through Baffin Island and down through the
province of Quebec and then into the United States.

"There may be some alternative methods of moving the
natural gas sooner, but those methods, all of them, are very
costly and their economics can't even touch a pipeline once
you get it laid."

The President laid down his notes, took off his glasses.
"On the basis of the advice of my experts, Monsieur le
Président"—he looked to those seated on his left and then
to those on his right and smiled—"and I could tell you
sometimes I wish I didn't have any experts and I wish I
hadn't taken their advice ... anyway, my experts advise me

that on the basis of the success of the under-ice experiments in the Byam Channel between Byam Martin Island and Melville, and on the basis of long-term economics, we will support the building of a pipeline from the Canadian Arctic Islands to the United States.

"While the pipeline is under construction, we'll just have to suffer as we have in the past. And I have to say this, if the Canadians had responded earlier by three or four years, the American people wouldn't be in this terrible crisis, we wouldn't have people freezing in the cold, we wouldn't have factories shutting down!"

Robert Porter bristled, colour coming immediately to his face. De Gaspé thought he was going to go after the President.

Instead, the Prime Minister kept his temper and conciliatory position. He said, "Monsieur le Président, as the President very well knows, my party and my government have been in power for only a short period of time. I understand his feelings of frustration in having to deal with the former government of Canada. But I must say I resent his trying to put on my shoulders the responsibility for negligence, default, or failure to give the United States what it needs in natural gas. If we're going to get anywhere in this bargaining, Monsieur le Président, I would respectfully suggest through you to the President that, before he starts another battle, he must understand he has just lost a war."

The President rose to the bait. "Now see here, Porter! Goddamn it . . ." He shook his fist in Porter's direction.

President Giscard d'Estaing intervened immediately. "Now gentlemen, please. I understand all the issues, all the emotions, but the question is what shall the transportation mode be? Mr. President, you have stated your choice in no uncertain terms." D'Estaing turned to Porter. "And what does the Prime Minister have to say in response?"

Robert Porter leaned forward on the conference table, left his operating file closed and referred to no notes. He looked at Giscard d'Estaing during his first few words, then turned to look the President of the United States in the eye. "Monsieur le Président, let me say that from the very beginning of the energy shortages in America, we in Canada have been and are very sympathetic to the crisis in which the people of the United States find themselves. The fact that the President as Commander-in-Chief of the United States Forces attempted a military annexation of Canada, failure though it was, has profoundly impressed me and my Cabinet and everyone in my nation. Fortunately, the people of Canada look upon that action as the act of one man, in isolation from the reality of the wishes, desires, and aspirations of the great people of the United States." Porter addressed the next remark to the President. "One would have thought, Mr. President, that the example of your immediate predecessor who took that kind of remote position might have been enough to stop you from taking military action against us."

Now it was time to be conciliatory.

The Prime Minister turned his head to address his remarks to the Chair. "Monsieur le Président, having said those things, let me say to you that not only do I understand fully the urgent need of the United States to have an enormous new supply of natural gas at the earliest possible moment, I also comprehend the American and, in particular, the Texas oil and gas people's love affair with the pipeline. All of them in the oil business, every one of them, is so enchanted with the pipe you'd think it had hair around it!"

There were a few snorts around the table at that remark. Porter paused for a moment.

"There are other methods of moving natural gas from the Arctic Islands. I'd like to review them very quickly before I state Canada's position on the President's proposal."

The President of France nodded his head in agreement, at which point Porter, for the first time opened his file and referred to his notes.

The American President leaned back in his chair, his hostile attitude somewhat diminished by Porter's apparent softening of attitude.

Wolf was taking notes.

Glasses now in place, Robert Porter said, "Monsieur le Président, I shall be very brief for the simple reason that the President and his advisors are fully aware of what the alternatives are. But it is necessary to state them for the record.

"If a pipeline is not used, then the alternative must be either submarine, aircraft, the lighter-than-air craft, or the tanker. Using any one of these four modes or any combination of them requires that the gas be liquified, that is to say, be reduced to 260 degrees below zero Fahrenheit. The liquid gas then must be placed in special, uncontaminated containers which also hold the cold. It is in these tanks that the commodity is transported.

"The lighter-than-air craft has many grave shortcomings as a long-distance or, for that matter, even short-distance hauler of bulk commodities especially in the Arctic where ice can be easily picked up on the surface of the craft."

The President of the United States, a skilled, experienced airman, nodded his agreement to that remark.

"In addition, they have relatively small payload and handle poorly in substantial winds. Nevertheless, a great deal of research has been going on with the dirigible particularly in the Soviet Union and in the United Kingdom. Even so, I would discount this vehicle for a high-volume, twenty-four-hours-a-day, reliable movement."

He waited for an objection from the President. There was none.

"The next is the submarine. General Dynamics Corporation of the U.S. have had on the drawing boards and in the experimental works for many years now a system of submarines of about 150,000 tons deadweight which could operate under the icepack in the Canadian Arctic Islands. They would take on their LNG* loads at special stations under water and under the ice, moving them out to open water ports at the eastern end of the Northwest passage, to ordinary LNG tankers which would take the commodity to designated American ports where it would be offloaded, gasified, and fed into normal domestic pipeline transmission systems.

"The next mode is the aircraft. Boeing has in production the huge resources carrier aircraft which is now committed to moving crude oil from Melville Island across to Prudhoe Bay where it is fed into the enlarged pipeline transmission system from Prudhoe Bay to Valdez, then into tankers for trans-shipment to the western seaboard of the lower United States. That aircraft, which has a pay load of over 2.3 million pounds, could also be readily adapted to a liquid natural gas movement following the same route."

President d'Estaing interrupted Prime Minister Porter. "You speak of a route which is not across or through Canada. I should have thought that you would want to utilize your own land mass for such a system?"

"Your point is well taken, Monsieur le Président. If I may, I will come back to it in a moment.

"There is already in existence a new but relatively small fleet of special Boeing 747s, which are freighters designed

*LNG – liquid natural gas.

93

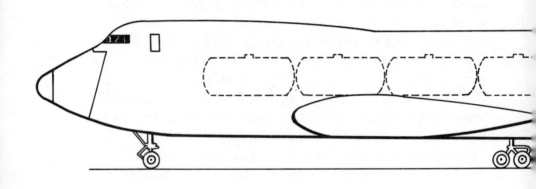

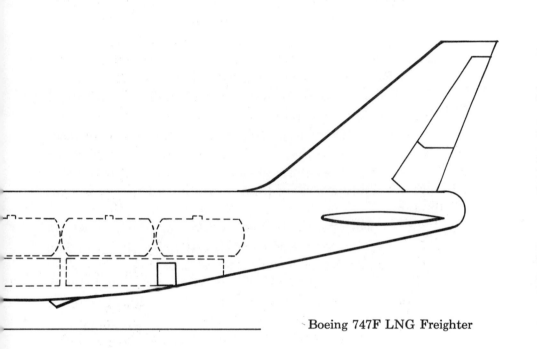

Boeing 747F LNG Freighter

specifically to carry liquid natural gas. These units are committed to a domestic Canadian movement of gas from King Christian Island where it is liquified and flown to an open water port on Devon Island at the east end of the Northwest Passage. There is is transferred into Class 10 ice-strengthened liquid-natural-gas tankers and then carried south through the Hudson Strait into Hudson Bay and James Bay, where it is discharged at a new deepwater harbour called Jamesport on the west coast of James Bay about thirty-five miles north of a place called Moosonee in northern Ontario. There the LNG is gasified, stripped of feedstock ingredients—there is a new petrochemical plant at Moosonee for that purpose—and the gas put into the normal distribution system for the southern Ontario/Quebec markets.

"The 747s operate in the system for the five winter months of the year when ice conditions in the Canadian Arctic Islands are such that not even Class 10 strengthened freighters can get through. The ice conditions coupled with total darkness make ship navigation impossible. There are six Class 10 LNG tankers in this system. The shipyards of the United States, France, the United Kingdom, and Japan could turn out many more in quick order.

"At King Christian Island, the gas liquefaction plant in operation there was constructed in the United States, assembled at Newport News on a specially designed series of barges and was successfully towed into the Arctic Islands and into position a year ago last summer—1979."

The U.S. President's patience was beginning to wear a little thin. "What are you going through this long shopping list for? We're prepared to build and pay for a pipeline system direct from the Arctic Islands. We'll do it ourselves. All *you* have to do is give us the right-of-way."

The Prime Minister shook his head in disagreement. "If

it were to be a pipeline, Mr. President, that pipeline would have to be owned and controlled in Canada and its construction and financing would have to be done by Canada. That would mean using your money and other world money in debt form. We'd have to bring it into Canada. And if we go for the pipeline, we have several other basic problems. The first is another settlement with the native people whose lands lie in its path. Then we would have another confrontation with those concerned about the damage to the ecology. And then there is the competition between Quebec, on the one hand, and Manitoba, on the other, for the pipe to come through their territories. In other words, a pipeline would be a divisive interest in a country which is already hanging together by its fingernails . . . although I must say, Mr. President, that your unhappy attempt to annex us last week has done wonders for national unity."

The Prime Minister turned and addressed his remarks to President Giscard d'Estaing. "Monsieur le Président, the reason that I have been going through the shopping list, as the President puts it, of alternative modes of transportation of natural gas from the Canadian Arctic Islands to the lower United States is simply that Canada cannot tolerate any further upward pressure on its dollar. That dollar has already been driven to $1.11 against U.S. currency, largely because of the infusion of foreign capital into Canada for the purpose of building the Mackenzie Valley pipeline. Of the $10 billion total capital requirement for that venture, $6.72 billion was spent in Canada for goods and services.

"In addition, over $8 billion has been spent on the James Bay project in the province of Quebec since 1973; some $12 billion for synthetic oil plants in the Athabaska Tar Sands in Alberta; and, in that same period of time, approximately $9 billion for nuclear generating plants for electricity and the heavy-water plants that go with them.

"The financing of this enormous capital investment has been through the money markets of the world. This input of foreign capital into Canada, when taken together with a continuing substantial trade surplus brought about by our sale of raw natural resources, has put our dollar in a high position. As a result, our secondary industries, our manufacturing firms whose goods must now be bought in the world market place at $1.11 U.S., when the same product can be bought from the United States for $1.00, are now priced right out of the market. We've faced with the shutting down of plants across Canada and unemployment in large scale at a time when our economy ought to be booming."

Robert Porter was speaking calmly, confidently.

"My advisors tell me that, in their opinion, if a pipeline is built from the Canadian Arctic Islands to the American border, the cost of it has got to be somewhere in the neighborhood of $12 billion and that the resultant strain on manpower, equipment, services, and supplies would drive prices even higher in Canada in a period of continuing escalation. But even more important, our dollar would very likely rise to $1.25 U.S. within the next two years. This would be totally unacceptable for Canada and would bring about the collapse of the industrial and manufacturing segment of our economy and destroy our grain and agricultural export markets.

"I'm sure the President and *his* enormously skilled advisors know exactly what I'm talking about."

The President remained silent.

The Prime Minister continued. "For all of these reasons, Monsieur le Président, the position of Canada is straightforward and simple. The United States can and will have access to the natural gas in the Canadian Arctic Islands, but the transportation system designed and built to carry it out of that region must be one built and paid for outside of Canada, whether that transportation system takes the form of submarines, aircraft, liquid natural gas tankers, or a combination of all of those modes.

"Furthermore, the gas liquefaction plants must also be built in some country other than Canada. The money for the capital expenditures for this transportation system, whatever form it takes, must be foreign capital and it must be expended in countries other than Canada.

"Tankers, aircraft, and submarines can be brought on stream and put into operation much quicker than the pipelines. Since time is of the essence for the people of the United States, who so desperately need the natural gas, I would have thought that the modes other than pipelines would have been highly attractive to the President."

The Prime Minister concluded. "For these reasons, Monsieur le Président, it is the position of Canada that a pipeline to deliver natural gas from the Canadian Arctic Islands to the lower United States cannot be permitted. On the other hand, we will do everything in our power to facilitate the development of port, navigation, air, and other facilities necessary to assist the United States to mount and operate a sea/air transportation system."

Robert Porter sat back in his chair, leaned toward Pierre de Gaspé, and asked if there was anything that he should add. In de Gaspé's opinion there was not.

The President of the United States remained silent for a few moments, contemplating the astute young Canadian Prime Minister across the table from him. This was not the time for a snap response.

The President did not ask advice of his people.

Finally he turned to Giscard d'Estaing and said, in his slowest Texas drawl, "Monsieur le Président, as I told you before this meeting started, I am in the middle of my re-election campaign and I must get away from here as fast as I can. I'm committed for a big kickoff dinner in Houston tonight, and I've got to stop at the White House on the way through to deal with urgent business."

The President of France nodded his head knowingly, a man in complete sympathy whose own re-election campaign days were not too far away.

"Yes, I could sit here and wrangle with you, Prime Minister, over these issues for the next two or three days, but I just haven't got the time and also it doesn't make sense. What does make sense is for me to recognize Canada's economic position and the danger of further erosion of its economy by driving the Canadian dollar up further. I can see that clear as a bell.

"And you're right. The oil company people do look at pipelines as if they had hair around them. It's time they changed their thinking and their pressure on people like me.

"Well, you've given us access to the natural gas up there in the Arctic, and you've set a reasonable wellhead price, and I think it's only fair that we go along with your transportation position."

Irving Wolf pulled at the President's sleeve, but was waved off. The President wished to conclude.

"The United States is most grateful to you, Monsieur le Président, for your most helpful, soothing presence at these important proceedings and for making this neutral meeting place available on such short notice. The friendship of the great people of France has always been and will continue to be treasured by the United States."

Then facing Prime Minister Robert Porter and at the same time standing up, the President said, "And Prime Minister, I would be less than honest if I didn't say to you that you have my admiration and respect, the respect of a

Texan, for the way you've handled yourself, not only today, but also during the events of last week. I only regret that I fell into the trap of all my predecessors in taking you and Canada for granted and not making a real effort to come to you and talk before I acted."

The United States
October/November, 1980

Immediately after leaving the St-Pierre et Miquelon conference on October 14, 1980, the President of the United States
had gone back to the campaign trail, travelling throughout
America claiming he had solved the natural gas shortage by
putting the Canadians over the barrel.

His challenger was the bright, articulate Senator from
Michigan, David Dennis, whose political base was in the
membership of the United Auto Workers of America. He
had served the interests of the auto workers as a hard-
bargaining labour lawyer during all of his remarkable professional career until politics–first as the Mayor of Detroit
and then as Senator–had taken him out of the practice of
law.

Dennis had taken the other side of the energy issue and
the confrontation with the Canadians, saying that the President got no more out of the Canadians by attacking them
than he Dennis could have done by accepting their perfectly reasonable offer to negotiate; the President had
humiliated America in the eyes of its own people and in the
eyes of the world by attempting to take Canada by force
and–what was worse–by failing.

David Dennis won the election.

Like the man he defeated, Dennis was tough and a hard
negotiator. A lean, lightly-built person of medium height,
the new President moved with agility and quickness. His

102

appearance and presence were commanding. His long, narrow face was dominated by deep-set almost grayish eyes and a head of black fringe-graying hair. His swarthy complexion provided a background to the magnificent white teeth which were often displayed by a man who smiled a great deal and enjoyed doing so.

David Dennis was a superb orator and a man who came across extremely effectively on television.

Dennis, the experienced politician, accepted as his political Golden Rule the principle attributed to Mahatma Ghandi. Ghandi's statement—and he used it often—was "There go my people. I must follow them for I am their leader."

David Dennis was indeed the new leader of the people of the United States of America.

He was also their first Jewish President.

Ottawa
Friday, January 23, 1981, 4:28 P.M.

The negotiations with the native people had gone well, a money settlement being arrived at similar to that of the U.S. government with the native people in Alaska, but in higher amounts. They would get $750 million in cash, sixty million acres of land in the Mackenzie Valley corridor, the Mackenzie Delta, and the Yukon; and a further $750 million to be paid out at the rate of a 2 per cent per annum royalty on gas and oil production from the area over a period of years. The money would go to co-operative corporations, owned and controlled by the native people according to their regions, with the proceeds to be used as they saw fit. The land would have to be selected by each co-operative group but could not include the pipeline rights-of-way or any roads or railway lines routes currently planned for the future. Any lands designated by the native people would be subject to expropriation by the Crown for the purpose of constructing roads, railways, or other transportation or communication facilities as are all other land holdings in the rest of Canada. These negotiations had been successfully completed by mid-January, 1981.

It was at this time, with the native settlement question out of the way and off the Prime Minister's mind, that Pierre de Gaspé decided it was the moment to approach him with the proposal for the take-over of Exxon.

The time was right.

The Americans had been sent home with their tails between their legs. The Canadian people were on top of the world and ready to take on anybody. The economy was booming. Substantial new crude oil discoveries continued to be made in both the Canadian Arctic Islands and the Mackenzie delta. Petro-Canada was expanding its exploration activities, but still had not been able to get into the business of refining and marketing petroleum products. De Gaspé desperately wanted to have refineries for the crude oil that Petro-Canada was producing as well as buying from off shore. But all such facilities in Canada were in the hands of the Big Six.*

If Petro-Canada could get into the retailing of fuel oil and gasoline, it could act as a competitive Canadian force to hold prices down. There was mounting public concern that the oil companies were ripping off the consumer. Gasoline in Ontario had gone from 69/70¢ a gallon in 1974 to $1.05 in 1981.

The next step in de Gaspé's thinking was rather than build a vertically integrated oil company, why not buy one. What better candidate for purchase than his old alma mater, Exxon Corporation, the biggest, the largest, the most powerful, and one which he knew well–the people at the top, the method and style of operation, its holdings throughout the world. His prime objective was to get his hands on Imperial Oil Limited, Exxon's Canadian subsidiary. Imperial was the major integrated oil corporation in Canada. It would be the ideal vehicle for Petro-Canada to control, but, in de Gaspé's judgment, the only way to get at Imperial Oil was for Petro-Canada to marry and carry off Imperial's parent, Exxon.

In the late afternoon on January 23, 1981, de Gaspé had

*Imperial (Exxon), Gulf, Texaco, Sun Oil, BP, and Shell.

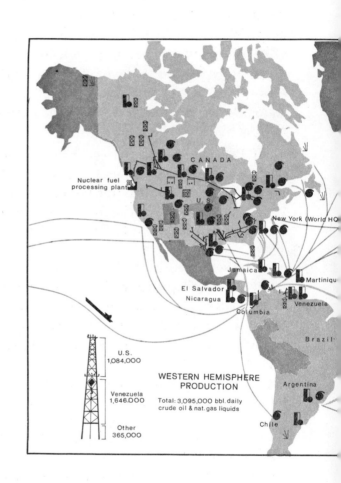

Nuclear fuel
processing plant

CANADA

U.S.

New York (World HQ)

Jamaica

El Salvador
Nicaragua

Columbia

Martiniqu

Venezuela

Brazil

Argentina

Chile

U.S.
1,084,000

Venezuela
1,646,000

Other
365,000

WESTERN HEMISPHERE
PRODUCTION

Total: 3,095,000 bbl. daily
crude oil & nat. gas liquids

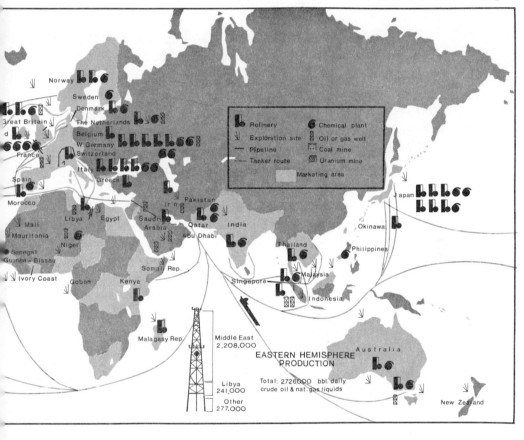

Norway

Sweden
Denmark
Great Britain
The Netherlands
Belgium
W. Germany
France
Switzerland
Italy
Spain
Greece
Morocco

Mali
Mauritania
Niger
Senegal
Guinea - Bissau
Ivory Coast
Gabon
Kenya

Libya
Egypt
Saudi
Arabia
Abu Dhabi
Somali Rep.

It n
Pakistan
Qatar
India

Japan
Okinawa

Thailand
Philippines

Singapore
Malaysia
Indonesia

Malagasy Rep.

Australia

New Zealand

b Refinery	**6** Chemical plant
↙ Exploration site	**8** Oil or gas well
— Pipeline	**□** Coal mine
⌐ Tanker route	**▨** Uranium mine
	Marketing area

Middle East
2,208,000

EASTERN HEMISPHERE
PRODUCTION

Total: 2,726,000 bbl. daily
crude oil & nat. gas liquids

Libya
241,000

Other
277,000

met with the Prime Minister in his office in the East Block of the Parliament Buildings. De Gaspé had opened by saying, "Prime Minister, I propose that Petro-Canada do a take-over bid on Exxon."

The Prime Minister, totally astonished, had responded, "Exxon? Pierre, you must be out of your mind."

"Maybe I am, but let me put my case to you, then make your decision."

The Prime Minister laughed, "Go ahead, but I think I should have a sedative before you start."

De Gaspé took from his briefcase two copies of his memorandum on Exxon. He handed one to the Prime Minister, who said, "I don't want to look at this. You tell me what the deal is and if I'm interested, I'll read it."

Porter leaned over, flicked on his intercom switch, and said, "Joan, hold my calls for the next few minutes, please. Okay, Pierre, now tell me all about Exxon. Exxon?!"

Pierre de Gaspé was very relaxed with the Prime Minister. Their friendship, which began at the time Porter first entered Parliament, had grown during Porter's time as Prime Minister. They had continued to see a great deal of each other, since certain major elements of Petro-Canada's policy-making process were in the hands of the Cabinet.

De Gaspé began. "First, let's look at why we should buy. Ever since the October war between the Egyptians and the Israelis back in 1973 and the resulting crude oil embargo, crude oil prices on the world market have gone up to fourteen dollars a barrel. The corporate profits of all of the major oil companies have escalated enormously. Sure, they'd had periods of low return, but the high prices of gasoline against enormous profits all combined to put the oil companies in a pretty bad light. And instead of holding the line, they've continued to jack up their prices, despite the fact that the cost of product in Canada has not escalated.

"Now, as you know, all of the vertically integrated major retailing oil companies in Canada are foreign owned. Five are owned in the United States and the sixth, BP, is owned in the United Kingdom. That means that the major policy decisions of all of these companies, including Imperial Oil which is Exxon, are taken at the foreign head office. I know the protests we get when we say this, but it's a fact. The major decisions of Imperial are made at the Exxon building in New York, including the appointment of Imperial's chairman and president.

"If Petro-Canada is to be an effective arm of government policy in keeping gasoline and fuel oil prices competitive, then we've got to have control in Canada of one of the major retailers. If oil company prices get out of line, we can put our product on the market at levels that will force the others down, but at the same time allow them a reasonable profit.

"So, my first reason is that PetroCan and Canada need to own or control one of the major gasoline and fuel oil retail companies.

"If the principle is accepted, then we've got two ways to go. One is to build and develop our own marketing company. That would entail buying service station sites, building our own stations, and developing the entire infrastructure. It would take an enormous effort and a long period of time.

"The other route is to take over one of the existing majors. I've examined the availability of the Canadian operation of all of them and, short of expropriation or nationalization—which you have said is unacceptable—the only way to go is by take-over bid on a foreign parent.

"Another reason for PetroCan's acquisition of a major Canadian oil company—let's call it Canadian at this time even though it's American owned—is that almost all of them are engaged in exploration work in the Mackenzie Delta, the Canadian Arctic Islands, Alberta, and offshore on the east coast. They're either alone or in partnership or in farm-out arrangements. PetroCan's exploration program, which is a development of Panarctic's original position, is doing very well, with continuing major gas discoveries and, more recently, the oil on Melville. But to have ownership of the wells and the exploration work and techniques of Imperial would be of enormous domestic assistance to Petro-Canada's objectives. And of course, Imperial is the largest retailer of petroleum products in Canada. If it were controlled by PetroCan, its marketing would have a profound influence on pricing practices throughout Canada."

The Prime Minister nodded in agreement. "Yes, the points you make are good ones, not bad at all. But what about Exxon itself? Why should we get involved in a world-wide operation such as theirs? . . . I think I know the reasons myself, and they already sound attractive to me, but let me hear what you think, Pierre."

"All right. If Canada buys Exxon, you automatically have control of an oil and chemical company that trades around the world from the position of an empire unto itself. Exxon has, in effect, a diplomatic interface with practically every country on this planet. It uses that interface for its own corporate purposes and also to further the interests of the United States. Clearly, that's the name of the game everywhere. In my opinion . . ."

The Prime Minister broke in. "It's your opinion I want, Pierre."

". . . Exxon, as a multi-national worldwide Canadian corporation would enhance our prestige everywhere. It would give us contact points in countries where even our External Affairs people aren't represented. And speaking of the External Affairs department, to have the Exxon trade-mark with a maple leaf in the centre of the "O" spread out throughout the United States, Europe, the Far East, and everywhere else Exxon operates would probably make them pick up their socks – and God knows they need it. I can remember back at the beginning of the seventies trying to get External Affairs to put an ambassador into Kuwait and one into Saudi Arabia and the rest of the Middle East countries. But no, they accredited our ambassador to Tehran to those countries much to the anger of the Arabs, who couldn't understand why Canada didn't know that the Iranians were not Arabs. For them the fact that our Ambassador to Tehran was also accredited to the adjacent Arab countries was a terrible insult. It still is."

De Gaspé checked with his memorandum. On to the next point. "On a worldwide basis, the cash flow from Exxon will be sufficient to do a pay-out of the acquisition cost plus carrying charges in less than ten years."

The Prime Minister stood up, turned, and looked out the window behind his desk, with his hands shoved in his pockets, he thought about the matter for a few moments.

Then he turned to face Pierre de Gaspé and said, slowly, "You know, Pierre, that's quite an idea. But tell me, how much is it going to cost?"

"We're going to have to find $20.5 billion to get 50.1 per cent. We'll have to borrow $14.5 billion of that outside Canada."

The Prime Minister was aghast. "My God, where can we find money like that?"

Pierre de Gaspé was ready. "I have a plan, sir. It's in the memorandum, and if you'll give me a minute, I'll go over it with you."

De Gaspé went over the figures carefully with the Prime Minister. When they were finished, Porter looked up and

111

said, "I like it, Pierre, but there's no way I'm going to make a decision on that one all by myself. Give me a shorter memorandum—even a handwritten one. Security on this will have to be tight. Don't make it any more than two pages if you can help it. Let me have it. I'll get my key people in Finance; Treasury Board; Energy, Mines and Resources; Industry, Trade and Commerce; and the Bank of Canada. I want you here, too. We'll sit down and kick it around." He checked his diary and with Tom Scott. "Right. We'll meet tomorrow morning at eleven o'clock—here."

De Gaspé had prepared his memorandum. The meeting had been pulled together as promised. He had been grilled for three hours. The result was unanimous: an enthusiastic approval of his scheme for the financing and execution of the Exxon take-over bid.

With the go-ahead approval wrapped up, de Gaspé moved quickly.

Obviously, financing was his first problem. There was no way he could look south across the border into the United States for that commodity. He had to go east, across the Atlantic to Switzerland and do business with the gnomes of Zurich.

Zurich
Thursday, March 12, 1981, 3:15 P.M.

By mid-afternoon on Thursday, March 12, 1981, a typical, misty drizzle had settled over Zurich.

Pierre de Gaspé looked out from his high hotel window across this grey, sombre city, the legendary home of the bankers known around the world as the "gnomes of Zurich." He was waiting impatiently for the international operator to report on his urgent telephone call to Canada.

During the past week, he had been negotiating with Swiss bankers on a continuing, almost around-the-clock basis. As the days had moved along, he had finally narrowed his discussions down to one, Credit Swiss, an ancient, conservative banking institution with enormous reserves and ready access to U.S. dollars.

This was not a conventional attempt to borrow. As president of Petro-Canada, his task was to arrange firm banking commitments to lend funds to Petro-Canada with its principal shareholder, the government of Canada, as guarantor.

At two o'clock that afternoon in the elegant, walnut-panelled office suite of Kurt Reimer, the president of Credit Swiss, the negotiations had been successfully completed with the signing of a memorandum outlining the basic terms of the deal that would give Petro-Canada and de Gaspé access to more than enough capital to finance the Canadian take-over of Exxon, the largest multi-national oil corporation in the world.

Immediately after the signing of the memorandum of agreement and a jovial celebration drink and toast with Kurt Reimer and his banking colleagues, de Gaspé had hurried to the privacy of his hotel room so he could report by telephone to the man who was his main supporter in the execution of this most grandiose of all take-over schemes.

De Gaspé had had several discussions with Robert Porter during the past few days when he needed instructions and advice. Because of the absolute need for maximum security, de Gaspé had taken on the negotiations single-handedly and, for the time being, had by-passed his own board of directors to deal directly with the Prime Minister.

At this moment, his jubilant euphoria at having pulled off this enormous financing deal made him tense and fidgety as he waited for the Prime Minister to call back. When the phone finally rang, de Gaspé leaped for it.

"We are ready with your call to Prime Minister Porter in Edmonton, Canada," the operator reported.

"How are you making out, Pierre?" came the clear, strong voice of the Prime Minister.

De Gaspé's response was loud and enthusiastic. "Terrific, Prime Minister. We've got a deal! It's done! We've just signed the memorandum of agreement."

The Prime Minister was delighted. "Congratulations, Pierre. Frankly I didn't think you'd be able to do it. You've been working against some of the best negotiators in the world for what has to be the biggest amount of money ever borrowed in one package. Now, if you can pull the rest of this deal off, it will be the greatest coup in financial history. It will be marvellous for Canada. Just incredible. What are your plans now?"

"I have to be back here in a week, next Thursday. The formal documentation will be ready for checking and signature by then. That'll give me time to get back to Canada to report in detail to you–"

114

Porter broke in, "And my Cabinet committee—"

"... and your Cabinet committee and to my own board of directors. My target is to be in Edmonton by Sunday night. I'd like to see you first thing Monday morning, sir. Is that possible?"

"I'm not sure, Pierre. I'll leave word for you at your hotel. Where will you be staying?"

"At the Château La Combe."

"Okay. Now, what does your timing look like on the take-over bid?"

"Well, the funds will be available to us whenever we're ready to go—that looks to me like a target date of the first of May. I'll need that kind of time to organize my legal documentation, set up both my Canadian and U.S. fiscal agents, prepare the documents for filing with the Securities Exchange Commission, and also finalize with the Canadian bankers."

The Prime Minister agreed. "You'll need that kind of time—no doubt about it. The House of Commons will be back in Ottawa by then. Just as well, because there'll be a hell of a commotion when we let this one go."

"You better believe it!" de Gaspé laughed. "I'm off to London now. I just might do a little celebrating tonight."

"Why not," said Robert Porter. "After all, it isn't every day that a fellow arranges to borrow $14.5 billion. Your pals at Exxon are going to go right out of their minds the day Canada bids to take them over. See you here Monday morning."

Edmonton
Monday, March 17, 1981, 9:30 A.M.

Pierre de Gaspé knocked gently on the door of the Prime Minister's suite in the Macdonald Hotel in Edmonton. Robert Porter had arranged to see him after breakfast at 9:30. He would be able to see de Gaspé for an hour.

The door was opened by Tom Scott, the Prime Minister's principal secretary. The two men exchanged familiar greetings as Scott took de Gaspé's coat. They moved into the suite's main sitting room which had been turned into an office area with desks, filing cabinets, telephones, stacks of files and papers, and three secretaries, two of whom were attractive young things, a fact not missed by Pierre de Gaspé as he took in the scene. The third was a rather senior lady, grey-haired, glasses, plump, with a pleasant warm face, Joan Michaels, the Prime Minister's longtime secretary who had been with him through thick and thin. After de Gaspé's words of greeting with her, Tom Scott explained the set-up.

"The P.M. is using the bedroom over on the right as his private office. We've had the bed taken out, and a desk and telephone and all the other good things installed temporarily. His own personal suite is the Royal Suite at the end of the hall on this floor. As you can see, we've got teletype, television on a closed circuit with Ottawa through the satellite Anik IV, and in his office we've got the red hot line telephone which puts him in touch with the usual people on the international map."

116

Scott checked his watch. "He should be along in about ten minutes, Pierre. He's meeting with the Cabinet in the sitting room of his own suite which is doubling as the Cabinet room. We've got a long table set up. It's working very well. He didn't tell me what you're seeing him about. Sounds to me like a deep, dark secret."

De Gaspé smiled lightly, "Yes, it sure is a deep, dark secret and I hope to hell it stays that way until we have a chance to put it all together."

He waved his hand in a circular motion, around the room, and asked, "Tell me, Tom, how is this concept of a mobile House of Commons working out in practice?"

Scott's head nodded positively. "It's going very well. Much better than I thought it would and I think a lot better than the P.M. had hoped for." He took de Gaspé by the arm, "Come on, let's go into his office, we can sit and have a chat for a minute before he gets here."

Scott led the way, asking one of the younger secretaries for coffee, which was quickly produced for them after they had settled down in Porter's office.

De Gaspé was well versed on the theory which brought the House of Commons to Edmonton for the first of many sittings at major regional cities across Canada. Porter had persuaded the Commons that 114 years after Confederation it was time to make some drastic changes in the form and style of Parliament without going through tedious efforts to obtain amendments to the British North America Act.* It seemed that changes in the B.N.A. Act could never be brought about because of a continuing inability to get the provincial governments together on a common ground with the federal government.

Porter's "Mobile House of Commons" concept did not

*Appendix II, page 211

117

require any change to the constitution. What it needed to bring it off was a little imagination, some inconvenience, and the unlocking of the House of Commons from the hallowed and never-challenged belief that it should sit only in Ottawa.

Tom Scott continued. "As I said, it's going very well. There've been some communications gaps but nothing really serious. The ministers and deputies can keep in constant touch with their offices in Ottawa and their staffs there. We have a closed-circuit television net which allows them to deal directly with their own people virtually face to face. The telecommunications system is good and so are the telephones, obviously. So they've been able to keep up and keep on doing business with no problem at all. In fact, I think they're having a ball."

De Gaspé was curious. "And what about the press reaction?"

"Well, by and large, an excellent reception." Scott had a pleased smile on his face. "And the people of Alberta seem to think it's great. We've also got many Members of the House, particularly those from Ontario, Quebec, and the Maritimes, who've never been to the West. I can tell you they're getting their eyes opened in this city and in the surrounding region. They've been out looking at the gas and oil fields. They've been into the Rockies. They've talked to people. It's been quite an experience and I think one hell of a good one."

Without warning, the Prime Minister entered the office, moving quickly, as usual. Pierre de Gaspé jumped to his feet as the two men greeted each other warmly, the Prime Minister enthusiastically patting de Gaspé on the shoulder while shaking his hand.

"It's great to see you, Pierre, or maybe I should call you moneybags."

He laughed, "Not yet, Prime Minister. We've got the money but we haven't bought anything."

"Well," said the Prime Minister, directing de Gaspé to a chair opposite his desk, as he went around it to take up his own seat, "there's only one person in Canada who can put this deal together. You're it. And frankly, I'd have been damned disappointed if you hadn't pulled it off in Europe."

The Prime Minister turned to Scott who was still standing and said, "Tom, I wonder if you'd leave Pierre and me alone. We've got one or two important things to discuss that I don't want to bother you about at this time."

Scott smiled, said, "Yes, sir," and promptly left the room, shutting the door quietly behind him.

The Prime Minister leaned back in his leather swivel chair and said, "Well now, Pierre, I want to hear all about the Zurich exercise and your big deal there." A knock on the door signalled the production of coffee.

De Gaspé gave Porter a comprehensive detailed report on the negotiations, the memorandum which had been signed, and an outline of the next steps and the pattern toward launching the take-over bid on Friday the first of May.

When Pierre was finished, Porter said, "All right, I want you to be prepared to make a presentation to the ... what I call the 'take-over' committee of the Cabinet. I don't want any more than the gang you met with earlier to have any knowledge of what's going on. That's the Ministers of Finance; Energy, Mines and Resources; Trade and Commerce; President of the Treasury Board; Governor of the Bank of Canada. And again, nothing in writing.

"I suggest you give us this briefing immediately after you've settled your arrangements with both your Canadian and American fiscal agents. You'll need their opinions on the bid price and the layout of the finalized scheme. When you have that information, that'll be the time to talk with us and we'll give you a final 'go' or 'no go.'"

The Prime Minister took a sip of coffee. "When do you think you'll be back to me?" he asked.

De Gaspé thought for a minute, pulled out his diary, stuck on his glasses, plowed through the pages, and announced, "The twenty-sixth–ten days from now. It won't take too long to get both the Canadian and U.S. fiscal agents organized. I've laid out a plan of action I think they'll probably buy anyhow."

The Prime Minister snorted. "Knowing you, I'm sure you've got the whole thing set up in a way that they'll be happy to follow."

"I do my best," de Gaspé replied. "If you can give me a time during the twenty-sixth, I'll set up my own PetroCan board for a meeting in the afternoon or immediately following your Cabinet meeting."

The Prime Minister reached over to flick his intercom button and said, "Tom, March twenty-sixth–what does ten A.M. look like for a one-hour meeting."

The response was immediate. "It's okay, sir."

"Good. Line up Finance, Energy, Treasury Board, Trade and Commerce, Bank of Canada–just the Ministers and the Governor of the Bank. No one else, please."

"Yes, sir."

Porter turned back to de Gaspé. "That's it, Pierre, you're on. It's organized."

"One final thing, Prime Minister, the Canadian agent I propose is Fry Mills Spence Limited. If you have no objection, I'd like to use them."

The Prime Minister smiled, "You have my blessing. The Fry Mills firm, like all financial houses in Canada, is politically acceptable if you understand what I mean."

De Gaspé returned the smile. "I knew they were when I

asked them if they'd be prepared to take part in a large deal—subject to your approval.

"And in the States, Morgan Stanley has been the fiscal agent for both the government of Canada and Exxon Corporation so they couldn't act because of a conflict. In my view, there's only one logical candidate and that's Merrill, Lynch, Pierce, Fenner and Smith. They've got the background and institutional contacts; they're spread right across the country, and they're international."

"Press on, Pierre, the Canadian oil industry needs some Exxoneration," he laughed, "if I may be permitted the privilege of coining a word."

Toronto
Tuesday, March 17, 1981 8:00 P.M.

De Gaspé shut the door of his Royal York Hotel suite behind the first of his two visitors. As Paul Zimet was hanging his coat in the hall closet, de Gaspé apologized to him. "Sorry to drag you out for one of these long evening meetings, Paul, but I have no choice as you'll soon find out. I've got one more person coming I didn't tell you about– Hubert Peters of Merrill Lynch."

Paul Zimet's eyebrows lifted in an involuntary show of surprise. In the investment fraternity the best know the best, and as a senior vice-president of Fry, Mills, Spence Limited and one of Canada's top oil investment experts, Zimet knew them all.

"Good Christ, Pierre, you must really have something hot going for you to bring Peters to Toronto," he said. "He's got to be top dog in the United States in oil securities. Why the hell would you have him here?"

De Gaspé chortled, "Eat your heart out, Zimet. You don't know what I've got up my sleeve, and neither does Peters. But when I'm finished with you people tonight, you'll have been through one of the great evenings of your lifetime. I guarantee you'll be in a state of shock."

"Try me," quipped Zimet, as he made his way to the conference table temporarily set up in the middle of the sitting room.

At that point, the legendary Hubert Peters arrived to be greeted by de Gaspé who then introduced him to Zimet.

122

The balding Peters, with his portly contours and hanging jowls, presented quite a contrast to the youthful Zimet, whose reddish-blond hair was stylishly cut and whose eyes were clear and alert. Peters, in his late fifties, looked a mess, but his facile, experienced brain was in fine shape.

"I can see you're wondering what Zimet is doing here, Hubert," de Gaspé said to him. "Well, I can tell you he was wondering the same thing about you. I have an idea you're going to see quite a bit of each other in the next few weeks, if what I have in mind is acceptable to both of you. Well, gentlemen, shall we sit down and get going."

De Gaspé took the head of the table. To his right he had a blackboard set up so any of them could explain a point graphically but without leaving any record.

"Now then gentlemen, in the folders I have here," and de Gaspé patted the stack by his right hand, "I have all the basic information on the world's largest multi-national American controlled oil company – Exxon.

"I have carefully checked out both of your firms, and I am satisfied that there is not conflict of interest which could be raised if you agree tonight to act as agents for Petro-Canada, backed by the government of Canada, in a take-over bid on Exxon. That is why I have brought you here – to ask if you will act as our agents. You've already taken a pledge to secrecy. What I want to ask you now is whether either one of you is aware of any impediment which would prevent your firm from acting."

Zimet asked in an astonished tone, "Exxon? Are you sure you don't mean Imperial Oil?"

"No way," de Gaspé replied. "I mean Exxon – which obviously includes its 70 per cent interest in Imperial Oil."

Hubert Peters was stunned. He said, "I know the Exxon situation inside out. Do you have any idea what a take-over bid would cost? How much of the stock are you looking for?"

"I'll come to those questions when we've got the answer to the question I put to both of you. I'll put it another way. Is there any reason why you could not act as agents, and if there is not, are your prepared to act? What about it, Paul?"

Paul Zimet had regained some of his cool. "The answer, Pierre, is there is no impediment to our acting. We would be privileged to be a part of the deal."

De Gaspé was pleased. "Excellent," he said. Then he turned to Peters. "And what about Merrill Lynch?"

Hubert Peters looked uncomfortable. He hesitated, then said quietly, "We are prepared to act as your agent in the United States. There is no impediment I'm aware of that would prevent us from doing so, but—I've got to say this—as an American I believe in my country. I think it's the finest in the world. I think Exxon is the finest oil company in the world. It's American, even though it's multi-national and operates in virtually every country of the globe. So I've got to tell you in my gut I feel like a traitor to my country when I say 'yes,' but I say yes anyhow." He raised his right hand slightly in a cautionary way. "And frankly, Pierre, just another gut reaction. I think you're going to have a hell of a fight on your hands from the Exxon board—and from every goddamn politician in the United States. Well, anyhow, Merrill Lynch will act as your agent in the United States subject, of course, to knowing what the proposal is and whether we think it's a workable deal."

De Gaspé smiled with satisfaction. "I'm delighted, Hubert, and I agree with you. I think we're going to have one hell of a fight on our hands, but in my view it's going to be worth it."

Hubert Peters came right back at him, "Yeah, but why take on the whole Exxon thing? Why not just go after Imperial Oil?"

124

"Simple. Exxon's not about to sell its 70 per cent interest in Imperial, and the government of Canada is not about to expropriate the 70 per cent interest. Yet we want Imperial and we also want access to the world's markets for our surplus oil. With the enormous finds in the high Arctic we have an opportunity to export to western Europe, Japan, anywhere we can find a market. And the government believes that it is in the best interest of the people of Canada to have a Canadian oil-based multi-national corporation interfacing with as much of the world as possible.

"Because Exxon is so large in Canada – it predominates in our domestic market and in exploration and discoveries – it's the logical choice to go after. But again, not by expropriation or nationalization. We have to use the take-over route."

De Gaspé was emphatic. "The decision has been made to go. We've done all our homework."

Peters shrugged his shoulders, "Okay. So we go."

De Gaspé passed around the thick folders. "At the top of each of these you'll find a two-page memorandum which sets out the basic parameters of the proposal. The rest of the stuff is background material which each of you has in your own research files anyhow. What I want to do is review this memorandum with you, answer your basic questions, then give the two of you forty-eight hours to come back to me with your suggested modifications to this plan and your joint proposals as to how the bid can be successfully engineered."

Zimet and Peters extracted the material. De Gaspé waited until they were organized.

"Let me run through this memorandum quickly with you. The bid will be for 50.1 per cent of the outstanding shares of Exxon. There are presently 236,643,000 shares issued and outstanding. The bid should be at a 10 per cent premium at current market values. That puts the bid price at $170 a share. I think 10 per cent is sufficient to flush out 50.1 per cent.

"At $170 a share, 50.1 per cent will cost us $20,325,224,-310 rounded to $20.5 billion plus your commissions."

Zimet exclaimed, "Jesus Christ! Where in the hell are you going to find that kind of money? That's impossible!"

De Gaspé smiled, but his voice was slightly hard as he shot back, "It's not impossible. I've got it all arranged. If I didn't have it all arranged, I wouldn't have you here.

"Petro-Canada is in for two billion; the government will put in another two; the Canadian banks will advance two; and the balance has been negotiated with the Credit Swiss Bank in Zurich and will be available in U.S. dollars as required. The background material in the file provides that information and all details sufficient for both of you to be able to assess the viability of the proposal and for your lawyers to be able to put together the necessary documents for filing with the Securities and Exchange Commission."

Hubert Peters shook his head in amazement and then turned to de Gaspé and said, "If your bid is successful, what happens to the Exxon management?"

"Good question. Again, you'll find the answer in the supporting material, but it goes this way. The existing management, top to bottom, will be invited to continue, including the current chairman. I would become the vice-chairman and the majority of the board of directors would be carefully selected Canadians. I have a slate in mind that the Prime Minister has already approved. There would be an executive committee of the board made up of five people, two Canadians, two Americans and myself. The Americans would, of course, represent the interests of the 49.9 per cent of the shareholdings that we did not take out."

Peters nodded silently in agreement.

"Over a period of time, the head office of the company would be moved to Canada. I have in mind Calgary. The current head office building in New York would become the main operations office. Through the natural growth of Exxon it would take up the sectors of the building vacated by the executive and administrative move to Calgary. It follows that the head office of PetroCan will also be moved to Calgary and be on the same site as the Exxon head office.

"But let me make it perfectly clear, this acquisition of Exxon is much more than just an investment such as the Canada Development Corporation made in Texasgulf back in 1973. If we get control of Exxon, it will mean policy-making control, control over management, and putting the corporation on a worldwide direction which will benefit Canada, the country that controls it."

General discussion went on for another two hours, during which strategy, tactics, fees, the take-over bid chain of command, banking, preparation of material for filing, lawyers and who they were to be, date of the making of the bid, acquisition of Exxon shares on the market in advance of the bid, and other questions were raised and settled.

A major decision was taken to set up a take-over bid headquarters in New York inside the Merrill Lynch office. Hubert Peters of Merrill Lynch would mastermind the preparation of the scheme and its execution in the United States; and Fry Mills Spence, while they were performing the same function for the Canadian operation, would use the New York headquarters for the co-ordination and liason necessary to bring the take-over to a successful conclusion.

"Well, gentlemen," de Gaspé said at the end of the two hours, "we're just about finished for this opening session, but remember we've got, or at least I have, a critical deadline which all of us have to meet. Nine days from now, I have to report to the Prime Minister and his take-over bid

127

committee of Ministers to get their approval of what you people and I, the three of us, are going to put together for the mechanics of the take-over bid. And immediately following that meeting, assuming we get approval, I have to face my own board of directors.

"Now how long will it take you two to put a comprehensive plan together?"

Peters responded, "Well, I don't know about Paul, but if I can get my butt back to New York, get my hands on my research people and a computer, I can be back to you within seventy-two hours with a comprehensive plan. In fact, I don't see any reason why Paul and I can't have our joint plan ready within that period of time. What do you think, Paul?"

Zimet agreed. "From my end, the deal won't be nearly so complicated because of the few shares of Exxon held in Canada. I'll get together with our research people first thing tomorrow morning, spend the day at it, and then go down to New York tomorrow night. Then I'll move in with Merrill Lynch and Hubert."

De Gaspé was happy. "Sounds good, gentlemen. Sounds good. Let's set a time to meet back here. Say ten in the morning on Saturday, four days from now?"

"God, Saturday again," Zimet remarked. "My wife will kill me. Don't you ever spend any time at home, Pierre?"

"As a matter of fact very little these days," he said.

There was an uncomfortable pause until de Gaspé, pulling his thoughts together, said, "Now the final thing is this! Security is an absolute essential. My question is going to be, Hubert, how can we cover up or disguise the work that's going on in your offices and this whole scheme. For example, could you appear to be examining a take-over of Shell Canada which is 85 per cent held in New York, and appear to be using Exxon information for comparison purposes? Think about it."

"Sounds feasible," Peters agreed.

"If you have to have anything typed, refer to Exxon as Company Y, or for that matter, just leave the name blank. Even secretaries have big mouths. I don't have to remind you that if this deal blows because somebody in one of your firms leaks it, or no matter where the leak comes from, you people will lose out on the biggest commission ever paid for a single transaction."

As Pierre de Gaspé stood up to conclude the meeting, Hubert Peters had the parting shot, "Even brokers sometimes make a living by keeping their mouths shut. Our business is built on it."

Toronto
Thursday, March 26, 1981, 4:10 P.M.

Pierre de Gaspé looked down the long table past the faces of the full board of Petro-Canada to his chairman at the far end. All twenty-one faces showed that de Gaspé had their complete and undivided attention. He could see they had been knocked out by his request for approval of the Exxon bid, which the Prime Minister and his Cabinet committee had approved that morning in Ottawa.

This emergency meeting of the Petro-Canada board was held in a special room of the Royal York Hotel in Toronto. It was much more convenient for the board members who had to fly in from all over Canada to come to Toronto rather than out-of-the-way Ottawa. De Gaspé had come directly from his meeting in Ottawa in ample time for the board meeting which had started at 2:30 P.M.

He had first outlined to his board the arrangements made for Swiss bank financing, the participation of the government, and the take-over bid scheme (which de Gaspé now referred to as the Merrill-Fry proposal).

There had been questions—the most pointed of them coming from Senator Margaret Cameron. He now moved to the conclusion of his presentation.

"Mr. Chairman, ladies and gentlemen of the board, I've attempted in a fairly short period of time to place before you all of the background and all of the facts behind the proposed take-over bid of Exxon by Petro-Canada. This is, as I have said, the largest take-over bid in history, and it's bound to have an enormous impact, politically and publicly, in the United States. That country is especially sensitive since their humiliation by Canada last October.

"If you do approve of the proposition, the take-over bid date will begin on Friday, May first. We will need every moment of the month in between to prepare the bid documents, the filings with the Securities and Exchange Commission, and an effective public-relations program which will be launched at the same time as the take-over bid. Of course, the main focus of that program will be in the United States.

"So what I am asking for, Mr. Chairman, is approval to proceed with the take-over bid on Exxon as proposed in the material which has been submitted to you. I also ask, by the way, that none of this documentation be taken away."

The chairman nodded and said, "Thank you, Pierre." Then to the board. "Are there any further questions."

De Gaspé sat back in his chair and waited.

Senator Margaret Cameron's hand was raised instantly and recognized by the chair. She had only recently been appointed to the Senate, after her party had been defeated in the provincial election in Nova Scotia where she had been deputy premier. Not only had her party lost but she had lost her seat in the legislature as well. Rumour had it, and Pierre de Gaspé had good access to rumours in the Ottawa mill, that the widower Prime Minister, Robert Porter, had been seeing a great deal of her—some people thought in more ways than one—after they first met during the ultimatum crisis, when Margaret Cameron had represented the absent Premier of Nova Scotia at the emergency meetings with the Prime Minister.

Some people were sure that the two of them were spending weekends together, but de Gaspé didn't think that was possible. Robert Porter, while a very discreet man, was totally in the public eye and thus had no privacy at all. And if they had shacked up together, at least for any period of time, the press would have been on to it in an instant.

It had also not escaped de Gaspé's notice that Margaret Cameron was a good-looking woman, with her flashing green eyes, red hair, and pink, smooth complexion—a real Scottish beauty. "If the P.M. had privileges with her, well, good luck to him," he thought as she began to speak.

Her soft but authoritative voice brought him back from his speculation, but not before he agreed with himself on a plan. She was staying in the hotel on the same floor as he. De Gaspé had booked in for the night. Maybe she would have a drink with him . . .

The meeting had been adjourned with approval to proceed, unanimously granted by the board. Even Margaret Cameron had voted in favour, notwithstanding her cross-examination of de Gaspé as to why the take-over of Exxon would be in the public interest for Canada. Immediately the meeting broke up, de Gaspé moved as quickly as he politely could to intercept her before she left the room.

Margaret Cameron was moving toward the door by herself when he touched her arm from behind. She turned, looked up at him, gave him a broad smile, "I hope you didn't mind my going after you."

De Gaspé looked down at her handsome face and returned the smile. "Senator Cameron, you asked a lot of questions which I'm sure I didn't answer fully, or to your total satisfaction. I'd like to pursue them a little further. Having made that statement, my question is whether you would join me for a drink in the Library Bar in about half an hour."

His mock, tongue-in-cheek seriousness and formality amused her.

"Pierre, I'd be glad to take you on – if you would pardon the expression. See you in the lobby in half an hour."

Each was prompt. They went in to the darkened Library Bar where Pierre's good friend, the maitre d', Caesar, placed them in a corner side-by-side table in the softly lighted room. Two gentleman-sized martinis relaxed them. It became increasingly clear to both of them that their obvious mutual attraction was not limited to their wide-ranging intellects and common interests.

As they started on their third round of martinis, Margaret touched de Gaspé's arm gently with her right hand, then left it there as she spoke to him.

He was acutely aware of that touch. It carried a message.

"Pierre, we've talked about the Exxon bid, and we've talked about all the good things it will do for Canada, and we've talked about the future of PetroCan. But you haven't asked me how I got on the board, although you probably have guessed . . ."

Pierre's shoulders lifted slightly as he interjected. "Well, the word around is that the Prime Minister has a soft spot in his heart for you, and when you lost your seat in Nova Scotia – you know which seat I'm talking about – two of the things he was able to do for you, and one hears there might have been other things as well, were to appoint you to the Senate and to the board of PetroCan. I might say that that was one of his better movements on the day he did it, or perhaps I should say actions. Anyhow, I'm delighted because you're here and I'm more relaxed than I've been in weeks."

There was a gentle squeeze on his arm as she said, "And I'm delighted to be here also. You know, there are some rumours about you also. But what really interests me is how you got involved in this whole thing. Here you are,

133

thirty-nine years old, tall, dark and handsome, and enormously intelligent and well educated. What made you start on this project? What is it that drives you to put together the biggest take-over deal ever?"

De Gaspé picked up his martini glass in his right hand and looked into it with a long gaze.

"I can't tell you, Margaret. It's just my nature. I can see things that have to be done, at least I think they have to be done. There are opportunities to do things, concepts which emerge, needs that have to be filled, so I go and do the things I can. It's my nature, I guess. The way my genes are put together. But I often get the feeling when I see something that should be done – something that should be built, deals that should be made – if I don't do it no one's going to do it. So I get the bug and there's nothing I can do to turn it off. I just have to do it, or at least try to do it, because I fail as often as I succeed."

He turned to look at her for a moment, and took her hand in his. "There's another thing too. As you go through life you collect certain experiences, a certain education, a certain background, and each of these things is a sort of block on which your ability to conceive or accomplish things builds. I have a hell of a lot more building blocks now than I had ten years ago and certainly fifteen years ago. I just have to use them, that's all. I just can't throw them away, or let them go to waste."

"Keep going," she said, "I'm interested. There are certain personal questions I won't ask you. But I'm interested in you and what makes you tick." She had not tried to withdraw her hand from his. As she spoke, he looked into her green eyes which danced brightly even in the semidarkness. He nodded and took a sip from his martini glass.

"I suppose as much as anything I'm interested in influencing the course of events, whatever that means. How can I have a hand in, or influence on where this country – or the world, for that matter – is going? To me that's most important. Can I do something in my work or in my profession that will be significant, that will help the people of my country, maybe even get me a little recognition or prestige in passing?"

Margaret broke in. "And to do what you've done, are doing, or what I'm doing, requires perhaps just a little bit more than a small ego, or translated another way, a small belief in one's own self and one's confidence and capability. What the hell, you've got to have confidence in yourself."

Pierre responded. "Absolutely. I want to be where the action is. I want to be in the centre of things, and why? Well, because there is satisfaction, a personal satisfaction in achieving an objective whether it's thinking up an idea or building something. It's the whole business of saying, 'My God, here's an idea – let's look at the idea. It's a good idea. And now, having had the idea, let's do it. Let's execute it.'"

Another sip of the martini.

"You know, Margaret, there are goddamn few people who have an idea and then put the idea into being, or into practice. Damn few. I've heard hundreds of people say, 'You know, I had that idea once, but I never did anything about it.' Sure, there are lots of ideas I have that I never get around to executing. One of my drives, one of the monkeys on my back, is that I'm a compulsive doer of things. If I have an idea I've got to try to carry it out. Not all of them, but most of them if they're any good at all."

Margaret squeezed the hand holding hers. "Speaking of ideas, you mentioned dinner. I think it would be a marvellous idea if we executed that one right now."

They both laughed. "Great idea," said Pierre, finishing off his martini.

An effusive Caesar escorted them the few steps to the

135

entrance of the Imperial Room where he delivered them into the hands of Louis, the famous maitre d' of the most elegant eating and entertainment place in Canada. Louis, an astute, discreet man, sized up the appearance of his valued client, Pierre de Gaspé, cast his eye around his vast room, then led the couple, as had Caesar, to a side-by-side table in the corner, not too far from the stage area. He seated them with the caution that he would return to make sure the service was to their satisfaction.

During the dinner, Pierre said to Margaret, "Look, I'm being personal, but one hears that your relationship with the Prime Minister is really very close. I mean there's nothing wrong with that, but if it is close—how can I put it—if it is close, is it also exclusive?"

She laughed and took his hand again under the table. "How sweet of you to ask. My relationship with the Prime Minister is a nice, comfortable one. We like each other a great deal and enjoy each other's company. It's a close relationship, but it is neither intimate nor exclusive." She paused. "Does that please you?"

He smiled. "Very much."

She went on, "And please understand that I know a lot about you. About your personal life, about your background. I've made it a point to find out, so I don't have to ask you any questions, nor do I intend to. I like you as you are, as you can tell."

After the floor show, they danced and talked about themselves.

Later as they moved from the elevator toward the door of her suite, Margaret looked up Pierre and said, "I'd like you to join me for a night cap, would you?"

"Well . . ."

"Come on now. I know you have a big day ahead of you in New York, but it's only eleven o'clock."

De Gaspé looked down into the green eyes of this most attractive woman. "What I was going to say before you interrupted me was that there is no way I would refuse your offer."

She had a fresh bottle of Courvoisier cognac, a favourite of Pierre's. There was more talk and more brandy.

He finally stood up and said, "Margaret, I really must go, it's after midnight. I have to be up at six to catch the plane for New York."

As she stood up beside him, he bent down and kissed her.

"Pierre, stay with me," she whispered.

New York City
Friday, May 1, 1981, 3:10 P.M.

It was 3:10 on Friday, May 1, 1981, as Pierre de Gaspé and his American agent, Hubert Peters, got out of their cab at the entrance to the tall, linear Exxon building on the Avenue of the Americas in New York City. De Gaspé stopped to look up along the pronounced vertical lines of the beautiful structure which housed the corporate headquarters of the most powerful, most productive, multi-national oil corporation in the world.

It was a warm, pleasant spring afternoon with an unusually clear sky above Manhattan, letting in sunlight unhampered by either cloud or smog. The glare from the windows of the top of the building where he would soon be meeting with George Shaw made de Gaspé squint his eyes.

He wondered, as he had many times before this day, what the reaction of his old mentor and now chairman of Exxon, George Shaw, would be when de Gaspé dropped his take-over bomb shell.

As he and Peters walked quickly towards the main entrance, their briefcases in hand, de Gaspé said nothing but his mind was racing with anxiety. He was, in fact, nervous. If he hadn't known George Shaw so well, and had such a close relationship with him, Pierre would have been his normal self, but Shaw's response was too important to him for too many reasons. And he knew that he was about to give the chairman of Exxon probably the biggest surprise of his life.

138

Having gone through two security checks and a final clearance to the executive suite on the top floor, de Gaspé and Peters were met by Shaw's secretary. She had been with him for over twenty years and was obviously, as was her boss, fond of Pierre de Gaspé. She escorted them directly to George Shaw's office where Shaw greeted de Gaspé affectionately and Peters, whom he had met during several negotiating sessions in the past, cordially.

After a discussion between Shaw and de Gaspé about their respective wives and de Gaspé's children, it was time for business. Shaw led them to the lounge area of the office rather than to his desk.

As he sat back in his special easy chair, he said, "Well now, Pierre, three-fifteen on a Friday afternoon is a bad time for an appointment, but I know that if you wanted to see me it had to be important. How can I help you?"

Pierre de Gaspé was sitting nervously on the edge of the sofa.

"George," he replied, "I want to come directly to the point. At five minutes past three, Petro-Canada, with Merrill Lynch as its American fiscal agent, launched a bid for 50.1 per cent of the outstanding shares of Exxon."

The colour quickly drained from George Shaw's face as a look of complete astonishment took over the comfortable, pleased countenance he'd worn just a second or two before. He gripped the arms of his chair and hauled himself to his full height.

He gasped, "You must be joking."

De Gaspé stood up to face him. "I'm not joking, George. A circular letter of offering has just been mailed to every shareholder of record. I'm here to inform you of the situation and to say to you that I hope that your board will regard this as a friendly take-over bid, because, George, we want your whole team to stay on. We have no intention of changing management."

139

Shaw walked over to his desk where he sat heavily in his chair, reached for the intercom button for his secretary and said, "Dorothy, ask Robertson to come in, please, as quickly as possible. Have him drop anything he's doing. I need him right now." Craig Robertson, another of Shaw's protégés, was now his president. They shared adjoining office suites. In a matter of a few seconds Robertson arrived and was perfunctorily introduced to de Gaspé, whom he had met years before, and to Peters.

"I thought you should hear this with me, Craig. I've just been informed by Pierre that Petro-Canada with the backing of the Canadian government has just launched a takeover bid on Exxon." Like Shaw, Robertson was practically overcome with appalled astonishment. For the moment he was speechless.

Shaw turned to de Gaspé and said, "All right, Pierre, you've told me that you want this to be a friendly take-over and you want management to stay on, but before we get into those details do you expect me to believe that Petro-Canada and the government of Canada are going to be able to find enough money to buy over 50 per cent of Exxon? I don't believe you."

De Gaspé responded quickly, as he fished into his briefcase. "The financing I completed on March tenth." He handed Shaw a document. "This is the offer which has been mailed to all of the shareholders of record. And, as you know, in accordance with the requirements of the Securities and Exchange Commission, we've had to make full and complete disclosure on all points. The offer expires at the close of business Monday, the eighteenth of May." He handed another copy to Robertson.

"Exxon has an authorized capital of 250 million common shares of which you now have 238,643,000 outstanding. In order to get 50.1 per cent, I have to buy 119,560,143. In the

140

past week the market range has been around $155 so we're offering $170 a share. Exxon stock performance has been poor in the past two years and a lot of people will want to get out. We believe that a 10 per cent premium will be sufficient to get the offering of shares that we want. The way I see it that will cost us about $20.5 billion."

Shaw broke in, "Okay. Now, I see from the financing statement that you've got two billion from the government of Canada, two billion from the sale of shares of PetroCan and a further two billion from the Canadian chartered banks on a two-year term, and the balance of 14.5 billion from the Credit Swiss Bank in Zurich. God knows whose money *that* is."

"Maybe only God knows, George, but I've got it against the guarantee of the government of Canada and I've got it for ten years at 10 per cent. That will be bringing home a lot of American dollars."

Robertson snorted, "That's about the only good thing I can see about it." He continued, "Listen, Mr. de Gaspé, perhaps I should, but I really don't know very much about Petro-Canada, not in depth anyhow. But doesn't the government of Canada own 45 per cent of its capital stock? In other words, isn't Petro-Canada a vehicle of the Canadian government? And if that's true, isn't this really a take-over of Exxon by the Canadian government? I'm going to tell you one thing, Mr. de Gaspe,"–de Gaspé could hear the hard ring of Robertson's Boston accent–"as the president of the world's largest oil and chemical complex, an American company through and through, which has done great service to the United States, to Canada, and to the entire world, and as an American citizen, I find it totally unacceptable and completely contrary to the national interest that Exxon should be controlled by foreign nationals, let alone by a foreign government and especially the government of

141

Canada, a country which is very little more than an economic colony of the United States."

Robertson was hurt, angry, and insulted. He stood up. "And let me say one thing more, Mr. de Gaspé, while I appreciate the courtesy of your coming here to tell us of this take-over bid, I for one am going to call an emergency meeting of the board of directors for tomorrow morning. I don't know what George is going to do, but I can tell you what I'm going to do. I'm going to ask the board to join me in fighting this take-over bid in every way we can—in the courts and in the Congress, if necessary."

New York City
Sunday, May 3, 1981, 2:00 P.M.

The news of the Canadian take-over bid on Exxon spread across the world almost instantly, stunning financial houses, enraging the corporate élite of the United States, and titillating millions of American citizens who had grown to despise the oil companies, good or bad. The news made proud, and perhaps a little bewildered, the people of Canada. Much like the woman who thinks she has a tumor but suddenly winds up giving birth to a child, Canadians were by and large enormously pleased.

And in Exxon countries around the world, where the friendly Canadians were applauded for having vanquished the Americans in the brief but stupid military incursion into Canada the prior October, there was even more delight in seeing the Canadian David once again taking on the U.S. Goliath with every possibility of success.

This was the largest take-over bid ever attempted. Its potential ramifications, the speculation as to the reasons behind Canada's move, the effects on Exxon management, the impact on the United States and its national interests, became instant newspaper fodder and headlines.

Throughout the United States, the editorial theme was consistent from New York to Los Angeles. The Canadian take-over bid on Exxon must be stopped at all costs because it would be against the national and international interests of the United States to have a foreign government in control of Exxon. Canada's use of Exxon would be in the national interests of Canada, not that of the shareholders. Furthermore, they feared Canada would cause the company to take steps that would further the interests of the Canadian nation rather than of the United States. In the presence of the increasing reliance on foreign crude oil and the continuing massive natural gas shortages, it would be critical for Exxon and the other major American-based, multinational oil corporations to do everything in their joint power to ensure the maintenance of an adequate supply of crude oil from the Middle East, Venezuela, and other sectors of the world. It was absolutely essential to the American national interest that the United States' share of Exxon's daily world production of 7.5 million barrels of crude oil not be diverted to Canada or be under the control of Canada to be diverted as it might direct.

A major sector of the Prudhoe Bay field in Alaska was owned by Exxon as well as major finds of oil and gas in the Mackenzie delta. The latter were under the name of Imperial Oil Limited, the Canadian subsidiary of Exxon. In order not to attract the attention of the average Canadian by reminding him that the largest, vertically integrated oil company in Canada was United States-controlled rather than Canadian, a decision had been made in 1972 not to change the name of Imperial to Exxon, although that change took place virtually everywhere else in the world.

Craig Robertson, president of Exxon Corporation, stepped out from the stage wings of the Exxon building screening room which sometimes, as on this occasion, doubled as the location for a press conference. He moved quickly to the lectern at the centre of the stage where he placed the statement from which he would read.

The room was jammed with people, taping machines,

television cameras, lights. This was an important moment for Robertson, who was about to announce the position of the board of directors and management on the Petro-Canada take-over bid.

Robertson was a diminutive man, with a round face and receding brown hair. Behind his black horn-rimmed glasses, his intense, piercing brown eyes gave some indication of his quick intellect. While small of stature, he possessed a presence and self-confidence which often bordered on arrogance. The product of a well-to-do Boston family, he had never known the sting of poverty nor the cut of failure. Throughout his years in school, culminating in a doctorate in chemical engineering, he was consistently at the top of his class. During his career with Standard Oil of New Jersey, later to become Exxon, Robertson had moved from position to position within the organization leaving a superior record of achievement and accomplishment behind him. As president of Exxon Chemical Company, while also serving as a vice-president of Exxon Corporation, he had overseen the development of many new plastics and had supervised improving the quality of Exxon's worldwide chemical business.

In 1978, George Shaw, as the new chairman of the board, had reached down the line beyond his senior vice-presidents to pick Robertson to be one of his two executive vice-presidents. Then in July, 1980, when the then president of Exxon had died suddenly of a heart attack at sixty-two, Shaw had moved up Robertson to succeed him.

The two of them, Shaw and Robertson, worked extremely well as a team, but there was no question that it was Shaw who was the chairman and chief executive officer of Exxon.

As Robertson walked onto the stage, his appearance caused some chattering among the reporters, most of whom had expected to see Shaw. But Shaw, although he was now

145

a United States citizen, had been born and raised a Canadian and so felt that Robertson should handle the press conference.

Robertson peered against the lights into the faces of the men and women, who sat poised with their pencils, pens, pads, cameras, and recorders ready. He waited a moment until the noise of discussion stopped and then began in his deep, strong voice, an unusual voice for such a small man.

"Ladies and gentlemen, on behalf of the board of directors and the senior executive group of the Exxon Corporation, I want to thank you for coming here on a Sunday afternoon when you could be out playing golf or," this with a devilish smile, "be in bed."

After the laughter had died down, Robertson went on. "The board and executive group of Exxon met in an emergency session yesterday morning and afternoon, and again this morning to work out a response to the Canadian takeover bid which was announced after the stock exchange closed on Friday afternoon. The board has authorized me to present this statement to you so the public can understand as quickly as possible, and before the stock market opens tomorrow morning, exactly where Exxon stands."

A voice from the audience to Robertson's left: "You mean, where the board of directors and the management group stand, don't you?"

Robertson tried to pick out the face that went with the voice, but couldn't do so in the smoke and lights. He replied, "Yes, that's true, but in a critical, urgent matter of this kind we have to manage in the best interests of the company just as we have to manage its day-to-day operations.

"Now if I can deal with the statement. Copies of it have been distributed. What I propose to do is go through it quickly and answer any questions."

Robertson read the statement rapidly, dealing first with

146

Petro-Canada's announcement on Friday and the visit of the president of PetroCan to Exxon to advise that the bid was on and that the intent was that management should remain. He then described the take-over bid as outlined in the stock offer documents filed with the United States Security and Exchange Commission. The offer was open until the close of trading on Monday, May 18, 1981, for 119,561,-000 common shares at $170 each. When he got to the meat of the statement, Robertson slowed his pace so the television and radio people could get a better audio coverage and impact. Robertson was an excellent speaker, well practiced and versed in appearing before television cameras and on the banquet circuit.

"The Exxon board and executive group are fully aware of, and in sympathy with, the national aspirations of Canada as it grows and develops and attempts to seek its rightful place as a major nation at the bargaining tables of the world. It is a country in which Exxon, through its subsidiary Imperial Oil Limited, has done business for many decades. Indeed, Imperial is the largest of all the integrated oil companies operating in Canada.

"If control of Exxon were to be taken over by an agency of a foreign government, Canada would have been our first choice because of the continued good relations between the two countries, notwithstanding the abortive and in our opinion ill-conceived attempt on the part of the former administration to forcibly annex Canada to the United States."

Robertson's voice rose as he put more emotion into his reading. "On the other hand, as the largest American-based multi-national oil corporation in the world, we believe that Exxon has a duty to more than just its shareholders. In our opinion, Exxon has a duty to the United States of America to do everything in its power to maintain ownership and

147

control in this country so that Exxon can continue to serve the goals, objectives, and interests of the people of the United States and not be diverted from that course by the assumption of control of Exxon by a foreign government, let alone by foreign nationals."

Robertson paused for effect. "What we are concerned with is a conflict of interest between the public policy and national interests of the United States and that of Canada, the foreign nation which would control the policies and indeed the management of Exxon for its own interests and purposes. In Canada's assumption of control of Exxon, we can see a real and direct threat to the continued supply of crude oil from our fields in Prudhoe Bay in Alaska and a real threat of diversion of a fundamental source of supply in Venezuela and as well the Middle East. Exxon now has a gross production of crude oil and natural gas liquids—together with crude oil off-take under special arrangements with other producers—which averages 7,500,-000 barrels a day. Refinery runs by Exxon and its affiliates average 6,400,000 barrels daily.

"The United States is an energy-starved nation, which depends heavily upon imported crude oil and petroleum products for its existence. To have the control of Exxon's massive, daily production in the hands of a foreign government constitutes, in our opinion," Robertson's right hand, index finger pointing Kennedy style, punched toward his audience for emphasis, "a threat to the national security of the United States.

"Exxon is not above the law, yet in many respects it is comparable to a nation unto itself with responsibilities which cross borders and are carried on the seas and in the air. Our total revenues last year were in excess of $30 billion—more than the revenues of the government which wishes to take us over.

"At this time, our attorneys are examining the offering circular. There are certain representations made in that document which may be worthy of challenge on behalf of the shareholders.

"In any event, we have instructed our attorneys to make application to the appropriate United States Federal District Court for a temporary order restraining Petro-Canada from proceeding with its take-over bid on the grounds that such take-over would be contrary to public policy and the national interest. If we are successful in that application, then a further application will be brought within a few days to continue that injunction and to ask for a preliminary injunction which would last until the trial of the issue. This application will be launched tomorrow morning."

Robertson noted with satisfaction that at least three reporters had gotten up to file hot copy.

"In addition, the management of Exxon will be sending a letter to all shareholders of record advising them not to tender their shares to Petro-Canada. That letter is in preparation and will be sent immediately.

"The third step that Exxon is taking relates to the fact that the courts of the United States have historically refused to prohibit the take-over of American-based multi-national corporations largely on the grounds that it would be inequitable for the United States to exclude a foreign corporation from taking over in the United States when United States corporations are doing exactly that abroad.

"The most recent example of a foreign take-over of a major United States multi-national corporation was a case not dissimilar to PetroCan's take-over bid on Exxon. This was the successful attempt of the Canada Development Corporation, a cousin of PetroCan, to buy 35 per cent of the issued stock in Texasgulf Inc., in the latter part of 1973. In that instance, the Canada Development Corporation

149

sought to acquire about ten million shares which would have given the CDC an effective controlling interest if management had viewed the bid as friendly. Management did not so view the bid and fought the take-over in the Federal District Court at Houston, Texas. In that application, the question of a possible conflict of interest on the part of the government of Canada and the Canada Development Corporation was raised and dealt with by the judge and upheld by an appeal court. The court held that the particular acquisition of Texasgulf by CDC was not contrary to the public policy of the United States nor against the national interest."

Robertson's mouth was getting dry. A sip of water. An adjustment of the glasses.

"Since the Texasgulf case there has been much discussion about the enactment of protective legislation to prevent take-over bids against the major or giant U.S. multinationals. No such legislation has been passed. The directors and executive group of Exxon corporation and countless others across the country believe that the time has now come when it is urgent and necessary in the public interest that prohibitive legislation be enacted by the Congress.

"In the interests of time, Exxon believes that if any legislation is to be passed, it should specifically deal with this crisis and not the whole general field of take-over bids against major firms.

"To this end, the chairman of Exxon corporation is meeting this afternoon with both the majority and minority leaders of the Senate and the House of Representatives.

"You should also know that our chairman and I will attend upon the President of the United States on Tuesday morning immediately after his return from his State visit to Israel. We have reason to believe that the President will support our request for prohibitive legislation."

The White House
Tuesday, May 5, 1981, 10:15 A.M.

The President of the United States greeted George Shaw and Craig Robertson cordially and motioned them to chairs in front of his desk in the famous Oval Office of the White House.

When they were all seated, the President said, "I understand you gentlemen have been in this room many times before doing business with the President of the United States, and I'm honoured to have you here on the occasion of your first visit with me."

Shaw responded, "We are obliged to you for seeing us so soon after your return from Israel, Mr. President. I gather your State visit went well?"

The President leaned back in his chair, smiling broadly. "Yes, indeed it went well. As you know I'm not an orthodox Jew—in fact a lot of people think I'm very unorthodox." His flat, nasal Detroit accent grated on Robertson's refined Harvard ears. "But for a Jewish boy from Detroit, a boy who's come up the hard way, to arrive in Israel as President of the most powerful democratic country in the world! Such a welcome! It was almost embarrassing. And I can tell you, gentlemen, I loved it."

The smile disappeared as the President leaned forward in his chair. "Mr. Shaw," he said, "you've asked to see me about Petro-Canada's take-over bid on Exxon. My staff have kept me abreast of the events that have occurred starting with last Friday when the bid was announced, but perhaps you can bring me up to date on what it is you want of me, although I assume you want my support for the prohibitive legislation you've already asked the leaders of the Senate and House of Representatives for.

"And if you do want my support, in all fairness, I think you ought to be prepared to make a very good case as to why I should give it, because I'm not at all sure I should."

Both Shaw and Robertson were considerably taken aback by the President's attitude. They had expected him to rally to the nationalistic cause and emphatically assert his support for their proposal.

It was Robertson who reacted first. "But Mr. President, perhaps you don't understand. Petro-Canada's take-over bid is in fact a take-over bid by the government of Canada. In other words, Exxon would come under the direct policy control of foreign government, which would clearly be in a position of acting contrary to the interests of the United States. Since Exxon is the largest oil company in the world and the United States relies on our crude oil production and refining capacity – I mean, Mr. President, it is in the national interest . . ."

The President held up his hand gesturing as if to slow down Robertson. "I understand the thesis you're putting forward, Mr. Robertson. Now I'm going to play the devil's advocate, but before I do so, you must remember that I personally am going to look at the situation through a different window than you two. First of all, both of you are at the top of the world's largest oil company. You're rich multimillionaires who are responsible to the shareholders of Exxon for managing the day-to-day affairs of the company subject to policy made by the board of your firm. You're well-educated gentlemen. You've lived in the almost royal milieu of the corporate élite of the United States for more

152

than two decades, each of you. Your responsibility is, as I said, to your shareholders, not to the people of the United States, although you are now attempting to create a responsibility to the American people in order to preserve your own management position, your own freedom of operation. In the United States you are not subject to direction or policy control by government, but you would be if the Canadians were successful in their take-over bid. You wouldn't like that and I don't blame you.

"On the other hand, that's a matter of corporate concern, not of public policy.

"The window from which I look at this scene has a different view. As you know, I'm a labour lawyer. For all of my professional career I have acted as counsel for labour unions, not for management but for labour unions in the toughest area of all, Detroit—and for the United Auto Workers in particular. My prime focus in life has been for the rights of the worker against corporate management— for the worker fighting for every buck and every privilege he can get out of the corporate élite. And so you must understand that my basic sympathies lie with the people, the workers of this country, and not with the handful of the citizenry who through private ownership or through corporations own the outstanding shares of Exxon."

The President caught Robertson's nervous look toward Shaw. "To gain my support, you will have to convince me that it is contrary to public policy and contrary to the national interest—that is to say, the interests of the people, not just the interest of Exxon and its shareholders—for the Canadians to be allowed to take control of Exxon.

"After all, Exxon and all the giant American corporations operate in virtually every country in the world. They have not been shut out except in certain places which have become violently anti-American or totally nationalistic.

153

Except for the Middle East – where the oil-producing countries have nationalized and taken over the oil companies' interests, including yours – you've had a pretty free hand all over the world as have all American based multi-national corporations.

"You know, if the Canadians *did* control Exxon, perhaps they'd keep their prices and profits down to a reasonable limit. A lot of Americans think the oil companies have been ripping off the public for years and that you've been working with other oil companies to control supplies and create shortages when shortages don't really exist. You know your credibility with the public is pretty low. As I say, maybe it would be a good idea to have the Canadians control one of our major oil companies. After all, every integrated oil company in Canada is American owned, except BP."

Shaw, who was becoming increasingly concerned that the President might argue himself into a negative corner, decided to attempt to change the line of discussion. He interjected, "Mr. President, it's quite clear that we've got some homework to do to convince you to support the prohibitive legislation. What we'd like to do is to come back in about a week's time and make a presentation to you and your advisors. Would you be prepared to give us this opportunity?"

David Dennis, the lawyer, skilled negotiator, and President, smiled. "Of course I would, Mr. Shaw. What I've attempted to do is to give you some insight into the kind of questions that are in my mind, not only questions, but attitudes. I think that my attitudes may well reflect those of a majority of the people in the United States.

"But instead of a week from now, why don't we leave it until the Federal Court has disposed of your application for a preliminary injunction. As I understand it, you're going to fight for the injunction on just about the same grounds you

154

want to convince me of. So if we leave your presentation until after the court has disposed of that application, I'll have the benefit not only of your proposals to me but of the thinking of the court as well. In fact, the court might uphold your position, in which event legislation might be unnecessary, although Congress may still think it desirable."

Shaw looked at Robertson, then turned to the President and said, "That would be acceptable, Mr. President, and makes good sense."

The President looked pleased. "Good," he said. "Now, before you leave, can you tell me what steps you've taken? I know that yesterday you got a temporary order restraining PetroCan from proceeding with its take-over bid, and that the court has set next Monday, the eleventh, for the commencement of the hearing for the preliminary injunction."

Robertson said, "That's correct, sir. We expect the hearing to last ten days to two weeks. We'll be calling expert witnesses, including some government people on the constitutional issues, on the question of national security and the national interest, and on public policy. I expect that PetroCan will be doing the same thing. In the meantime, shareholders of record are still able to tender their stock. Even though the temporary order is in effect, it does not stop the tendering of shares in response to PetroCan's offer. At this point we've found no serious defects in the representation made by PetroCan in the offering circular, so we're going to go strictly on the national interests and national security grounds.

"We have, however, sent out a letter to our shareholders advising them against tendering their shares to Petro-Canada. We've told them that we believe the current record price of Exxon shares is not realistic in view of the growing strength of the corporation and its diversified operations. We've made some new crude oil discoveries in the Mackenzie Delta which have yet to be proved up but our preliminary information indicates that our finds are going to be greater even than at Prudhoe Bay.

"We have pointed out the conflict of interest which we've discussed here this morning and have advised all of our shareholders—and most of them are American—that they should consider in their own conscience whether or not the tendering of their shares to PetroCan is unAmerican. We have advised that the board and management have concluded that the PetroCan offer is inadequate and not in the best interests of Exxon and its stock holders or in the best interests of the United States."

The President snorted, "That'll certainly make them think, but I'll make a bet with you, Mr. Robertson. My guess is that 50.1 per cent of the Exxon shares will have been tendered long before the expiry date. I hope you've been thinking about what you will do if my guess is right. Will you still proceed with the court action? Of course, the better question is, will you still want the prohibitive legislation when a majority of your shareholders are prepared to sell?"

Shaw concluded the discussion by saying, "Mr. President, we're considering those questions as any prudent businessmen would do. When we have to answer them, we will. Thank you for seeing us, Mr. President."

New York City
Monday, May 18, 1981, 12:24 P.M.

Judge Rupert Amory sat forward in his chair and tugged at his black gown. "Mr. Petroff," he said, you have informed me that your next witness will be the last one you will call for the applicant Exxon. Since it's almost twelve-thirty, I suggest the court might adjourn for lunch to reconvene at two o'clock. But before we do that there are certain matters that I would like to know about.

"First, how long do you think this next witness will take, Mr. Petroff? We've been at this for a week and I'd like to have some idea of how much longer we have to go on."

John Petroff, counsel for Exxon, rose to reply. "Your Honour, my last witness will be the president of Exxon, Mr. Craig Robertson. My estimate is that I will require this afternoon and most of tomorrow morning for my examination in-chief. My friend will probably require as much time for cross-examination but he can speak to that question."

Petroff sat down.

"Thank you, Mr. Petroff, and now, Mr. Day, how many witnesses will you call?"

Ambrose Day, the attorney for Petro-Canada, stood and replied, "Just one, Your Honour, the president of Petro-Canada who will give evidence on the background of the offer and the intent of Petro-Canada and the government of Canada in making the bid for control of Exxon. I will not call any witnesses in relation to the question of the United

157

States' national interest or conflict of interest or public policy because my client has instructed me that it does not wish to presume through witnesses or otherwise to argue as to the position that this court should take or indeed the government of this country should take in determining what is or is not contrary to the national interest or contrary to public policy of the United States."

Judge Amory nodded his approval, "I commend your client, Mr. Day, for a decision that is both wise and diplomatic."

The judge watched with some amusement the rapid scribbling of the host of reporters in the court room. This was news indeed.

"Well, gentlemen, it seems to me that with two more witnesses we should be able to complete this hearing by Thursday. If it is of any assistance to you, because of the importance of this matter and the urgency that a decision be handed down, I propose to have my judgment ready within five days after whatever day it is we conclude on.

"Also, I am aware of certain expressions of intention on the part of certain members of the Senate and the House of Representatives to put forward and support prohibitive legislation should the courts—that is to say, this court or any court above—fail or refuse to grant the injunction that the board of directors and management of Exxon seek. I can assure counsel that the possibility of the creation of such legislation will in no way affect my approach to the decision that I give, whatever it is."

Judge Amory paused for a moment, slipped on his glasses, took up his pen, and addressed himself to Ambrose Day. "Mr. Day, there is a matter of statistical information which is of interest to me. I do not propose that the information I wish should be placed on the record through a witness, but I'm prepared to accept it from counsel, although if

158

pressed by the other side, I'm prepared to entertain the evidence coming through a witness. But what I want to know is this – today is Monday, May eighteenth, the day on which Petro-Canada's offer to the shareholders of record of Exxon terminates. Quite apart from the matter of an extension of the time of the offer – and clearly because this application for an injunction has not yet been disposed of, there must be an extension offer by Petro-Canada – how many shares have been tendered so far? If I miss my guess, Mr. de Gaspé, whom I recognize as being in the courtroom, will probably have this figure up-to-date within the last half hour.

"If Mr. Petroff does not object, would you please inform yourself through Mr. de Gaspé as to the number of shares tendered to this time." Petroff, without getting up, shook his head in a negative way, indicating that he had no objection. "For the record, Mr. Petroff indicates he has no objection."

Ambrose Day, who had been standing during the judge's question, turned, looked into the audience, found Pierre de Gaspé in the second row, two seats removed from the centre aisle, went through the gate of the bar separating the audience from the attorneys, and met de Gaspé in the aisle where the two had a brief whispered conference. Then Day returned to the counsel table and still standing, said, "Your Honour, I'm informed by my client that at noon today, there have been tendered to the United States fiscal agents of my client 122,531,201 common shares of Exxon, which is substantially in excess of the 50.1 per cent. My client will, of course, acquire on a first-come, first-served basis the number of common shares of Exxon required to give Petro-Canada 50.1 per cent of all of the issued and outstanding common shares of Exxon. We anticipate late offerings which will, of course, be of interest to Petro-Canada."

159

Day turned for an instant to look back at Pierre de Gaspé who nodded his approval from the audience.

Day went on, "It follows, Your Honour, that an extension of the offer to purchase must be made by Petro-Canada to a date when it can be reasonably expected that these proceedings might be completed and your decision rendered and the matter of an appeal considered by each side, then launched or not launched. Also, in this case, each party must have an eye to what the Congress may do in terms of prohibitive legislation.

"Under the circumstances, my client considers it appropriate to extend the date of the offering to the shareholders of record on the same terms and conditions as heretofore have applied to be open until Monday, the first day of June. That extension means, of course, that those who have tendered their shares to this point are free to withdraw them up until June first. So therefore, Your Honour, while the figure I've given you is a valid one today, on June first it could well be that the number of common shares of Exxon then outstanding as tendered might be more or might be less."

The judge continued to make notes for a moment, then looking up toward Day, he remarked, "Quite right, Mr. Day."

"But from what you have told me it is apparent that the shareholders of Exxon, which are largely United States corporations and citizens, have decided that it is in their interests and–to the extent that one can interpret that decision–in the interests of the corporation that Petro-Canada's proposal should be accepted.

"That evidence should be of great significance to the board of directors and the executive group of Exxon and is of substantial importance to this court.

"This court is adjourned until two o'clock."

New York City
Tuesday, May 26, 1981, 7:22 A.M.

Pierre de Gaspé lay staring at the ceiling of his New York hotel room, eyes wide, but seeing nothing as the room slowly filled with brilliant morning light. His mind was racing, his body relaxed and comfortable with the warmth of the smooth, soft body of the sleeping Margaret Cameron nestled close up against him. But his mind was not on her. Instead, he was recapping, going back and forth over the quickly changing series of events of the past few days.

De Gaspé had come down to New York from Toronto on Wednesday, May 6, to be formally questioned in discovery proceedings by the attorneys for Exxon in preparation for the hearing in the Federal Court before Judge Rupert Amory which began in May 11. De Gaspé had intended to return to Canada immediately, but on the advice of Ambrose Day, Petro-Canada's New York attorney, he had decided to stay. It was just as well that he had. The need to make decisions and judgments, not only on the mounting pressure of the Exxon application for an injunction but on the acquisition of Exxon shares as well, had increased rapidly. He was the only one who could make those decisions and give instructions, either to the attorney, Day, or to Hubert Peters of Merrill Lynch.

As the emotional and nationalistic reactions to Petro-Canada's take-over bid on Exxon accelerated during the first few days after the bid was announced, de Gaspé had taken Peters' advice and accompanied him on quick visits to major holders of blocks of Exxon stock to assure them that PetroCan and the government of Canada would not attempt to cause Exxon to operate in any way detrimental to the interests of the United States, pointing out that the United States had so many opportunities for economic leverage and reprisals against Canada that it would be foolish for Canada to cut off crude oil or divert world supplies away from the United States or do anything that would be harmful to the American economy.

When the first of these major shareholders had tendered its stock, the event was widely publicized and encouraged other holders to put their shares forward.

By May 18, de Gaspé's maximum effort had paid off. Ambrose Day was able to advise Judge Amory that the number of shares tendered exceeded the required 50.1 per cent and tenders were still being received.

On the morning of Wednesday, May 20, Exxon had completed its case before Judge Amory. At that point Day had put de Gaspé, his only witness, in the box to outline the position of the government of Canada and Petro-Canada. In his examination-in-chief of de Gaspé, Ambrose Day limited his questions to Canada's objectives and took care not to ask any questions that would elicit from de Gaspé any opinion concerning the national interests of the United States or whether, in his opinion, control of Exxon by a foreign government could be detrimental to the national security of the United States.

However, John Petroff, counsel for Exxon, coursed back and forth over the difference in national interests of the government of Canada and that of the United States, citing Canada's early willingness to trade with Cuba and with Red China during the period when the United States had sealed off all doors to those countries, even though in 1981 the doors were wide open.

As a lawyer himself, de Gaspé had felt uncomfortable in the witness box. Petroff's questions were incisive and showed his intelligence and knowledge of his subject. De Gaspé could not help but admire the man.

De Gaspé had been the last witness. Petroff had called no evidence in reply. And so the case concluded late on Thursday, May 21, after both counsel had made argument.

In his concluding remarks Judge Amory stated that he would give his decision in writing at 10:00 A.M. on Tuesday, May 26.

The weekend had been hectic.

Late Thursday, Prime Minister Porter had sent a Canadian Forces Jet Star to pick up de Gaspé at La Guardia and take him directly to Ottawa where the House of Commons was again sitting. On Friday morning, he had met with the Prime Minister and his Cabinet committee and at the same time, with the executive committee of the board of directors of Petro-Canada which again included Senator Margaret Cameron.

His briefing of the group had been exhaustive.

On the question of which way Judge Amory would go, de Gaspé refused to give an opinion. He had great respect for the judge's background in corporate and constitutional law. In de Gaspé's view, he was an ideal choice to hear the case. There was, of course, an appeal to the appellate division of the U.S. Federal Court which could be taken by either side. It was likely if Exxon lost before Judge Amory, Exxon would appeal, which, of course, would further delay the completion of the take-over bid because undoubtedly the appeal court would continue the order restraining Petro-Canada from taking up and paying for the shares tendered.

De Gaspé's main concern was that even if Judge Amory's decision was favourable to PetroCan and the injunction was refused, the Congress might well enact specific prohibitive legislation. Some powerful members of both the Senate and the House of Representatives from both parties were making strong nationalistic and anti-Canadian speeches and promising support of a prohibitive bill.

But what was much more serious than mere talk was the fact that he had been informed, just before leaving New York that morning, that Senator Jacob Weinstein of New York, the Democratic majority leader in the Senate, and Congressman Albert Foss of Louisiana, the majority leader in the House of Representatives (the majority in both Houses being Democratic with a Democratic President in the White House) had announced that they would jointly sponsor an emergency bill to prevent the take-over of Exxon Corporation by Petro-Canada. It would be introduced in the House of Representatives, on May 27, the day after Judge Amory's decision, if that decision was against Exxon.

The Prime Minister remarked that it appeared to him that the Americans were almost panicking.

After answering a series of questions from the group, the Prime Minister closed off the meeting, saying he had to get into the House. However, he thought that it would be helpful to the committee of Cabinet and to the executive committee of Petro-Canada and to Pierre de Gaspé if de Gaspé had a liaison person from the joint group to work closely with him in New York in the last stages of the take-over operation. Porter had suggested Senator Margaret Cameron as the ideal person for the job and for obvious reasons he didn't think that Pierre would object to her presence. This with a smile.

De Gaspé had no idea whether the Prime Minister had any inkling of his relationship with Margaret Cameron, but he certainly did not object to the suggestion nor did Margaret Cameron.

Friday afternoon de Gaspé spent at his offices in Toronto. At home, Friday night, he had a flat-out fight with Ann, in which the names of Margaret Cameron and Dr. Rease, Ann's partner, were mentioned many times. Ann's new-found independence in her growing medical partnership and Pierre's indifference had brought both of them to the point of separation. De Gaspé packed and left that night. In fact, he had joined Margaret Cameron at the Royal York.

She had accompanied him back to New York on Saturday afternoon. Sunday morning they met with Hubert Peters and Paul Zimet at the PetroCan temporary headquarters in the Merrill, Lynch, Pierce, Fenner and Smith offices where Peters and Zimet of the Fry Mills Spence firm and their staffs were updating their statistics on shares tendered and certificates delivered. Only one block of 100,-000 shares had been withdrawn since the original closing date of May 1, while an additional 1,273,565 shares had been tendered after that date making a total offered of 59.3 per cent of the issued shares of Exxon.

From the viewpoint of an operation designed to gain control of the world's largest multi-national oil corporation without warning and by complete surprise, the exercise had gone perfectly, without a hitch.

Monday morning, May 25, de Gaspé had spent preparing for a press conference scheduled for 12:15 in a meeting room at his hotel. Lunch and drinks were served to the press before the one-hour conference had gotten under way at 12:45. De Gaspé and his advisors had felt it essential to make public for the benefit of the members of Congress the number of shares which had been tendered by the Exxon shareholders. They felt that the figure 59.3 per cent

165

would have an effect on the thinking of the members of Congress and on the board of directors and executive group of Exxon. This impressive tendering of shares would be a crucial factor for consideration by Exxon management if they had to make a decision to appeal from the as-yet undelivered judgment of Judge Rupert Amory. For clearly, by fighting the injunction, the management were no longer speaking for a majority of the shareholders of Exxon. If they were to win in their plea for an injunction, either at Judge Amory's level or in the appeal court, the take-over bid would be destroyed and very likely their future prospects with Exxon.

On Monday, May 25, the proceedings of Congress had opened against a background of television, radio, and press statements by Senator Weinstein and Representative Foss decrying Petro-Canada's take-over bid as being against the national interest of the United States and saying that they were prepared to put forward the Weinstein/Foss bill on Wednesday, May 27, if the decision of the court made it necessary that legislation be passed.

Senator Weinstein was a powerful figure in American politics and a highly respected senior member of the Senate. His reputation as a hard bargainer gave added force to his proposal. He made it clear on Monday that the Weinstein/Foss proposal was in two stages. The first stage would be a bill specifically designed to intercept and cut off the Petro-Canada take-over bid on Exxon. This was the key gut issue for the country and he felt that the bill would easily carry the House and the Senate. The bill would be short and sweet. Non-residents or foreign nationals – whether corporations, individuals, or foreign-controlled U.S. corporations – would be prohibited from voting or holding either directly or indirectly in the aggregate more than 25 per cent of the issued and outstanding voting shares of Exxon Corporation.

166

The second stage of the Weinstein/Foss plan was another bill to be introduced later in the Congressional session, but after the Exxon/PetroCan matter had been disposed of. This bill would similarly prevent the foreign acquisition of more than 25 per cent of the voting shares of any U.S. national or multi-national corporation with assets of over $5 billion as at December 31, 1980.

Weinstein and Foss, both of them old pros, could see that the second bill could get bogged down in debate, protracted committee hearings, and intense lobbying. That bill was for the long haul. The key political issue for the moment was Exxon and so they chose to cut their cloth to suit the occasion.

A major figure was yet to be heard from. The President of the United States, a Democratic President, a Jew from Detroit, sitting in the White House with a Democratic Congress, had not yet said what he would do with any bill, whether the Weinstein/Foss bill or any other legislation, that might be enacted by the Congress on the issue and placed before him for approval or veto.

As Pierre de Gaspé lay starting at the hotel room ceiling, his body breathing quickly but lightly, his brain focused on this question, what would the President do? What could he be expected to do, looking at his track record: labour lawyer for the United Auto Workers; a man always fighting against the big corporations and for the workers; and not known to be beholden to any major corporation at any time in any of his political career as Mayor of Detroit, Senator and now President?

During his election campaign, the President had pledged to the American people that he would conduct an open, aboveboard and public administration. He felt a strong obligation to keep the people of America informed as to his actions and had pledged that he would do so during his campaign.

167

Now that the Weinstein/Foss proposals for prohibitive legislation had been made public, speculation as to what the President would do was rising rapidly.

Pierre de Gaspé's mind was distracted momentarily by Margaret Cameron turning over in her sleep, intuitively moving her warm back into the curve of his body.

But speculation about what the President would do would be academic if Judge Rupert Amory came down against Petro-Canada and granted the injunction to the management of Exxon. Sure PetroCan could appeal, but that would take one, possibly two months, or even longer. A negative judgment by Amory, a distinguished, experienced jurist, skilled in corporate and constitutional law, would be end of the matter. No doubt about it. Pierre de Gaspé would soon have the answer to that question because at 10:00, in a little more than two and a half hours, Judge Amory would be entering his court room to deliver his decision. . . .

The telephone rang shrilly, startling de Gaspé and waking Margaret Cameron.

He lunged for the phone which was on his side of the bed.

"Yes?"

"Mr. de Gaspé?"

"Yes."

"Mr. de Gaspé, I'm sorry to call you so early in the morning. I hope you don't mind. You and I haven't met."

De Gaspé had already twigged to the voice.

"My name is Senator Weinstein."

"I recognized your voice, Senator. I've seen you on television a great deal in the last couple of days."

The Senator chuckled. "Good, good. Now, the reason I called is I think you and I should get together."

De Gaspé was startled. "Okay. When and where?"

"Your suite. Eight o'clock. What's that? I guess half and hour from now. Order me Sanka and a fruit cup. Gotta watch my weight."

New York City
Tuesday, May 26, 1981, 8:00 A.M.

Margaret Cameron had hurriedly dressed and gone to her own suite two floors below while Pierre de Gaspé ordered breakfast for Weinstein and himself, showered, shaved, and dressed.

The Senator arrived at 8:00 sharp, just as the breakfast appeared. While they were exchanging pleasantries, de Gaspé was impressed by the aura of confidence and power which literally exuded from this rotund New Yorker. A New Yorker he was, complete with the city's own accent. De Gaspé knew he was in his early sixties. He looked it, although he appeared fit, tanned, and well preserved.

When they had finished their meal, Weinstein pulled out a long, elegant cigar and said, "Hope you don't mind?"

"Not at all."

Weinstein lit it, sucking vigorously to get it going. "Yeah. Well, I guess we should get down to the short strokes. Today we hear what the court is going to say. If the Exxon management get their injunction, you're finished. You're out and Foss and I will not present the bill. I can't see you going for an appeal, or Exxon for that matter."

De Gaspé remained expressionless.

"Now if the court refuses the Exxon injunction, then Foss and I will introduce our bill tomorrow. It's sure to go through. As majority leader of the Senate, I guarantee it, and if Foss was here he'd say the same about the House. Okay?"

170

There was still no expression on de Gaspé's face.

The Senator went on. "So if the judge refuses the injunction, you look good, PetroCan looks good, and the Canadian government looks good—and the United States and Exxon lose face. And so, Foss and I introduce our bill. It goes through. The United States looks good. Exxon is preserved as it should be, as an American company, the largest oil company in the world. Canada and the Canadian government look bad; the relationship between the two countries, bad enough as it is now with that shambles last fall, will be in terrible condition again. Reprisals you know, the whole thing. Bad for both countries—very bad."

A long suck on the cigar, a great cloud of smoke billowing around de Gaspé, a non-smoker. Still no evidence of any emotion, or reaction.

"So what I'm saying is this—a deal." He spoke slowly now. "If the court refuses the Exxon application for an injunction, then Foss and I will not put forward our Exxon legislation if you agree to withdraw your offer to the shareholders. That way we can all back off and go home, and there won't be any confrontation between the two countries. God knows we've had enough of that."

Pierre de Gaspé coughed lightly from the cigar smoke, reached forward, and picked up the coffee pot. "More Sanka, Senator?"

"No thank you, Pierre." For the Senator everybody should be on a first-name basis, except when addressing the Senator.

"Senator," de Gaspé looked him squarely in the eye, "I've anticipated the proposition that you've just put to me so I got instructions from my government and from my board of directors on this very question last Friday. It might be an attractive proposition except for one thing."

"And what's that, Pierre?"

"You've got a President . . ."

The Senator broke in, "A fine President, a fine President, the best we've ever had. Fabulous guy and a Democrat and a Jew. My God, man, are we ever proud of him. He's honest and straight and free and not tied to anybody. A great man, a big man."

Pierre de Gaspé smiled, "Yes he is. And you've hit the nail right on the head. He's honest and he's not tied to anybody. He's the kind of guy who can make up his own mind, and he hasn't yet made up his mind as to whether he will veto or approve your bill. I don't care what leverage you've got on him, he's going to call the shot the way he sees it and he hasn't called it yet. Until he does, Senator, and until he calls it your way –"

The Senator's benign face hardened. He spat out with pure venom. "He'll call it our way or the son of a bitch will never get a goddamn proposal from the White House through the Senate again."

Suddenly the Senator's eyes shifted. His cigar turned slightly up as he kept it between his teeth. Then he took it from his mouth and smiled.

"On the other hand, Pierre baby, you may well be right. If you are, and he goes with you, there are a lot of us in Congress who owe a great deal to the oil companies in more ways than one, if you get what I mean, Pierre."

Yes, he knew what he meant, but said nothing.

The Senator went on, the smile still showing but the eyes ice-hard. "Now Pierre, there are two ways of getting at a young guy like you. One way is to use a little . . . how shall I put it . . . not blackmail, but a little bit of persuasion. Like, for example, a file on your relationship with Senator Margaret Cameron – complete with photographs – delivered to your wife." A puff on the cigar.

De Gaspé looked him right in the eye and said, "You rotten bastard."

172

The Senator tapped the ash off his cigar and said, "Relax, Pierre, relax. My personal file on you tells me two things. From your background, from the way you do business and from the way you handle yourself, you'd probably tell me to go to hell, and to send it to your wife anyway. The stakes are just too big.

"But my file also tells me that your wife already knows and that while you were in Toronto on the weekend, you and your wife called it quits. As a matter of fact, there has been a lot of screwing around – if you'll pardon the expression – on both sides."

De Gaspé's face was white with astonishment. "How in hell do you know? That was only last Friday."

The Senator chuckled, "Pierre baby, you're talking to the powerful Senator from New York. The Petro-Canada bid on Exxon is a matter of national security. You ever heard of the CIA, Pierre? They've got more stuff on their computer about you than you know yourself."

With that the Senator stood up, belched, walked to the closet, took out his tailored top coat and pearl grey homberg, and, with the cigar still clenched in mouth, put his hat on and said, "No, Pierre, that's not the way to deal with you. There's only one possible way I can get at you. I'm only going to say this once, so I want you to listen hard."

Weinstein's coat was on by this time. De Gaspé sat fixed in his chair.

The Senator said quietly, "You're the guy in the driver's seat. That's where you like to be and that's why I'm making this proposal. You make a formal request to come and see me and that dumb bastard Foss in the open – there will be press coverage – and you say that you've assessed the anti-take-over feeling in the Congress and you're certain that the bill is going to pass, and that the President will have no choice but to go along with the bill. You with me so far?

Then you say that in the interests of the relationship between two great countries—you know what to say, all that crap—Canada is going to withdraw its bid.

"Then if you do this, Pierre—and you've got to do it after the House has passed the bill but before it hits the Senate — then if you do this, Pierre baby, then there is two million dollars sitting for you in a numbered Swiss bank account. I'll give you the number after you've done your part of the deal. Think about it, Pierre baby. Think about it."

The Senator opened the door to leave and turned to de Gaspé for a final remark. "By the way, don't worry about this frank talk of ours. I took the precaution of having this place cased for bugs and taping equipment about two this morning. My people tell me that you and Maggie were so busy in bed you had no idea you had visitors.

"See ya, Pierre baby."

New York City
Tuesday, May 26, 1981, 11:00 A.M.

Judge Rupert Amory entered the courtroom directly from his chambers. Black robes flowing, he walked briskly to the steps leading to the dias and to his chair where, before being seated, he nodded to the counsel and audience who had risen on his entrance. He could see that the courtroom was jampacked again mainly with press people, their notebooks in hand. Television and other cameras were not permitted in this court, nor were recording machines.

The judge looked at the counsel tables in front of him. On his left was John Petroff, lead attorney for Exxon Corporation, who had with him today George Shaw and Craig Robertson of Exxon Corporation. The judge reflected that the presence of these two men showed that the Exxon management were taking this moment seriously, as indeed they should. At the counsel table on his right were Petro-Canada's attorney, Ambrose Day, and Pierre de Gaspé, the president of the corporation.

As Judge Amory sat down, and the people in the courtroom with him, he withdrew some papers from the large brown envelope he had carried into the courtroom with him.

The clerk of the court had called out the usual formal greeting, bringing the court into session.

Judge Amory waited for the people in the courtroom to settle down and then, glasses in hand, he made some preliminary remarks.

175

"Last Thursday, at the completion of the evidence and argument in the case of Exxon Corporation versus Petro-Canada, I stated that I would deliver my judgment this morning. I am now prepared to do so, but before I proceed further, I wish to compliment counsel on both sides for their superlative preparation and presentation of the evidence and their arguments. Their efforts have been of enormous value to me in the writing of this judgment, a judgment which will undoubtedly be the most important that I will be called upon to deliver during my career on the bench. The issue at stake, and the results of the determination of that issue, could have far-reaching effects relative to the ownership and control of American multi-national corporations which carry on business not only in the United States, which is their home country, but in one or more other nations throughout the world as well."

With this, Judge Rupert Amory put on his glasses, took up the text of his judgment, and began to read.

He dealt first with the background of the take-over offer, the financing of it, its compliance with the rules and regulations of the Securities and Exchange Commission, and the technical features of the circular in which the offer was made to the shareholders of record of Exxon. Then he dealt with the evidence of the expert witnesses for Exxon on the constitutional and corporate law of the United States, and as well the evidence of the president of Exxon, Craig Robertson. Next he dealt with the evidence of Pierre de Gaspé and with the arguments of counsel.

Judge Amory noted the percentage of the common stock, 59.3 per cent, which had been tendered to Petro-Canada by Exxon shareholders and he stressed his awareness of the expressed intent of the majority leaders of the Senate and House of Representatives to introduce prohibitive legislation should the court fail to allow the injunction applied for.

176

At this point in his judgment he said, "At no time should a court in the United States of America be put in a position by the legislative or executive branch of government where a decision of the court, or the judge making that decision, is publicly intimidated by a proposed legislative course of action. I wish to make it perfectly clear that I am not intimidated. On the other hand, as will appear from the reasons which I provide later in this judgment, it may well be appropriate that legislation is being contemplated."

This was a clue, rather a vague one, but sufficient to set up a slight chattering among the audience and between counsel and their clients.

The judge paused and waited for the discussion to subside. He used his gavel only on the rarest of occasions.

"As I perceive it, the real question before this court is what should the national policy be in protecting the national interests of the United States from the intrusion of a foreign multi-national corporation, owned or controlled by a foreign government, through its acquisition of an American multi-national corporation.

"To put the proposition another way, the question is whether the acquisition of control of Exxon, an American-based multi-national corporation and the world's largest oil corporation, by Petro-Canada is contrary to public policy and the national interest of the United States. The management of Exxon brought their application for a preliminary injunction on this sole, but enormously important point."

There was a distracting, short-lived commotion at the back of the courtroom. Judge Amory stopped, waited patiently until it subsided, then went on.

"Those who gave expert evidence for Exxon and especially Mr. McGarvey, a senior official of the State Department, who is particularly knowledgeable concerning the Middle East, were particularly informative. He said that through its arrangements with the various members of the Organization of Petroleum Exporting Countries, (such as Venezuela, Saudi Arabia, Libya, Kuwait, and others), and through its exploration work around the world, Exxon now controls the production of approximately 7,500,000 barrels of crude oil a day, a large proportion of which is shipped into the United States for consumption here. Also, the reliance of the United States on imported crude oil has risen from approximately 25 per cent of all crude oil consumed in this nation in 1973 to over 60 per cent today. It was his firm opinion, therefore, that any diversion to foreign markets, such as western Europe or Japan of crude oil now flowing under the Exxon banner into the United States could cause critical shortages of petroleum, fuel oil, and petroleum derivatives. He reasoned that if control of Exxon were to fall into the hands of a foreign government that government would likely use its control of Exxon to serve its own national interests in priority to the interests of the United States and that, accordingly, the acquisition of control of Exxon Corporation by Petro-Canada would be contrary to the public interest.

"I found Mr. McGarvey to be a strong and persuasive witness and I can find no reason to reject his cogent testimony."

Judge Amory paused for a moment, looked up and saw Petroff turn from his note-taking to whisper with a smile to George Shaw.

Judge Amory continued. "On the other hand, there is the real question of whether the issue of public policy and national interest as to the role of the multi-nationals should be decided by Congress, by legislation, and not by the court.

"To this date, the Congress of the United States has failed to enact legislation that gives guidance to the courts by settling in legislative form what is public policy and what is, or is not, in the national interest.

178

"This is so, notwithstanding the judgment of Judge Woodrow Seals in the case of Texasgulf Inc. vs Canada Development Corporation which was decided by the learned judge at Houston on September 5, 1973 and later confirmed by the Fifth U.S. Circuit Court of Appeals. The citation is 366F. Supp. 374 (1973).

"That case was not dissimilar to the one before me. As a result of a bid for 35 per cent of the issued and outstanding shares of Texasgulf Inc., made by the Canada Development Corporation, which historically is the corporate relation of the present respondent, Petro-Canada, the management of Texasgulf, a major multi-national mining firm with then approximately 65 per cent of its assets in Canada, applied to the court for an injunction restraining the Canada Development Corporation from proceeding with and completing its take-over bid.

"There were several grounds put forward in support of the application for the injunction, but in the result all of them were rejected and the application refused.

"One of the grounds relied upon by Texasgulf was the very question which confronts this court, that of public policy and the national interest. I quote from the lucid and well-reasoned judgment of Judge Seals which, in that it was upheld by the Circuit Court of Appeals, I consider to be binding upon me as a precedent. At page 418 he says this:

The court is aware that the issue of a possible conflict of interest also must be considered in a larger and broader context of public policy and national interest. That is, what should our national policy be in protecting the national interest of the American people from a real or an imaginary threat of the multi-national corporation, regardless if it is a private foreign corporation or one that is ostensibly a private corporation but nevertheless

179

is an instrument, directly or indirectly, of a foreign nation-state, such as the Japanese corporations who are now buying tracts of timber land and cotton fields in this country, or one such as Canada Development Corp. (which will sell to the Canadian public all but 10% of its common stock in the near future) and British Petroleum which is almost 50% owned by the government of Great Britain and has recently been reported to want to increase its ownership of Standard Oil of Ohio from a 25% interest to a 50% interest?

It seems to this court that if the threat is real, it makes little difference if the foreign multi-national is government owned and controlled or not. If it is government controlled, at least we will know 'our enemy' and to whom it owes this allegiance and through diplomacy and treaties could balance their political influence and their economic power. . . .

Perhaps these defenders of the multi-nationals are correct; that the entire world will benefit from an economic integration.

Be that as it may, we must realize that it is our [U.S.] multi-nationals who are the real giants – ITT, Xerox, Standard Oil, General Motors, Singer, Goodyear, IBM, Colgate-Palmolive, National Cash Register, Eastman Kodak, Minnesota Mining and Manufacturing, International Harvester, and many others.

Should we expect to operate freely around the world and exclude a foreign corporation such as CDC?

The answer of this court *in this case* is no. This particular acquisition is not a threat to the U.S. In fact, it might be, that if their acquisition is thwarted, our long-time friend, neighbour and ally, who we all know is now experiencing an increasing feeling of economic nationalism, might look to other methods of expressing this growing sense of economic nationalism.

It is an issue of public policy and national interest as to the role multi-nationals will play in the future, but this court cannot decide generally in the context of this case what this role may be. It belongs in the legislative and executive branches of government. This broad issue is too fraught with economic subtleties and questions of delicate balances of trade, as well as problems of economic reciprocity. Remember, turn about is fair play.

Suffice to say this case is not the vehicle to wander into this bog of uncertainty.

Of course, what makes this problem so pertinent now is the constant and continuous devaluation of the U.S. dollar, the depressed stock prices of many U.S. companies and the long period of unfavourable balances of trade. These factors emphasize and multiply this whole issue.

There are many good buys today in the U.S. by foreign-held American dollars as well as by foreign currencies. This acquisition, eventually successful or not, will not be the last one and especially from Canada where it is said that the U.S. controls 60% of their mining industry and 80% of their smelting and refining capacity. The CDC emphasizes that this acquisition would help our balance of trade to the extent of $290 million.

How can a court of law or equity even consider a problem so complex, hard and difficult? Only the Congress or the executive branch has the resources to determine what is in the best interest of this country in the increasing problems of multi-nationals.

Judge Amory hitched up his gown again, paused, took a sip of water, and looked around the courtroom at the furiously scribbling reporters.

"I have no choice but to agree with the reasons set forth

by Judge Seals when he says, 'Only the Congress or the executive branch has the resources to determine what is in the best interest of this country in the increasing problems of multi-nationals.'

"If I were to decide that the acquisition of control of Exxon by Petro-Canada is contrary to the national interest, or contrary to the national policy, I would be making a decision on a question of fact and not of law because neither the Congress nor the executive branch has enunciated the law. In this court, the law is interpreted, not made."

The judge could feel and hear the increasing tension in the court. He read quickly now.

"For the above reasons my decision in this case is as follows: the original temporary restraining order I granted on May 4, which allowed depositaries to continue to receive stock but has restrained Petro-Canada from further solicitation or taking up and paying for stock tendered pending outcome of this case, will continue for ten days to allow the applicant, if it so chooses to launch an appeal.

He paused for a moment. "The application by Exxon Corporation for a preliminary injunction against Petro-Canada is refused."

A stunned silence filled the courtroom for a moment –then bedlam.

Pierre de Gaspé was still at the counsel table with his attorney when he was interrupted by Hubert Peters. "Congratulations, Pierre, you must be really pleased."

"Congratulations to you, Hubert. You've done a fantastic job for us."

"Yes, but we're a long way from finished yet. We still have the Congress and the President ahead of us. Pierre, the president of the Credit Swiss Bank wants to speak with you urgently. They gave me the message when I called the office just a couple of minutes ago. Let's go to my office; you can call him from there."

When Kurt Reimer came on the line from Zurich, de Gaspé could hear him clearly. "First, how did the injunction go, Pierre?"

"Perfectly. The application was dismissed."

"Excellent! Excellent! Well done. You and your people have done a superb job." He paused. "But we have a problem."

With those words Pierre de Gaspé's victory euphoria suddenly faded. Reimer went on. "My principals are very much concerned that the Congress will pass prohibitive legislation and that the President will approve of it. It may be late in the day, but my people want to renegotiate one or two major points. They think their proposals will provide the final leverage you need to get by the President. They can meet you in London. Can you come over immediately?"

De Gaspé's reply was instantaneous. "Of course I can, Kurt. I'll catch a flight this evening."

"I've already made your hotel booking – at the Stafford, of course."

"Good. I hope we can get this over with quickly. I want to have a meeting with Weinstein at his Senate office first thing Thursday morning before the Weinstein/Foss bill is introduced in the Senate. I expect the bill will go to the House of Representatives tomorrow for emergency debate. It should pass. Then it goes to the Senate the next morning and quite possibly to the President that afternoon. The President still hasn't declared himself and he won't until he sees what Congress is going to do with it. And he's promised the Exxon people another shot at him to convince him as to why he should approve the bill, assuming it gets through Congress."

Reimer responded. "Well, there's still a chance. As I say, I think you and your corporation and your government will find the new proposals acceptable. While Canada might wind up in a different position in this deal, I'm confident its basic objectives can be satisfactorily met. See you tomorrow."

De Gaspé broke in quickly, "Kurt, before you go – I want to bring Senator Margaret Cameron with me. She's the liaison person for the Cabinet and executive committee of the board of PetroCan." In his mind's eye de Gaspé could see Reimer smiling.

"I'll book a separate room for her, Pierre."

"Thanks a lot. One final thing Kurt. Could you check through your old-boys bankers net to see if there's been a numbered account set up in Zurich in the last seven days. I don't want to know who or any details. I just want to know if it's been set up. The amount is two million . . ."

Margaret Cameron and de Gaspé had caught an overnight Pan Am 747 which put them into London shortly after 8:00 the next morning. They went directly to the Stafford Hotel on St. James Place, just behind the Ritz and just a short distance away from Buckingham Palance. The Stafford, a small elegant establishment, was, as usual, fully booked, but Simon Broome, the managing director and long-time friend of Pierre de Gaspé, had given up his own bedroom to de Gaspé and a last-minute cancellation had opened up space for Margaret Cameron.

After the commotion of their arrival – de Gaspé, the big Canadian, was a special favourite of the concierge, the porters, and especially of Louis and Charles, the French barmen in the delightful little room at the rear of the building on Blueball Yard – de Gaspé had checked with Kurt Reimer, who was at the Dorchester. He had agreed that they would have lunch at the Stafford with Reimer and his as-yet undisclosed principal. After agreeing to meet for a drink at 12:45, Senator Cameron and de Gaspé went to their respective bedrooms for some much needed sleep.

They met at the appointed hour in Louis' and Charles' small, very English bar, both of them much refreshed. A fast Vodka martini for Margaret and a gin and tonic for de Gaspé were ordered as they perched on stools at the bar.

"I suggested to Kurt that we could use your room for our discussions. Hope you don't mind, Margaret."

185

She laughed. "Not at all. I don't remember the last time I had three men in my bedroom at once, but I think I can cope."

De Gaspé gave her his best leer. "You don't need three, sweetheart, I can take care of you all by myself." At that moment he caught Charles totally absorbed in their conversation, taking in every look, gesture, and word. Charles knew Mrs. de Gaspé well, and he couldn't put these goings on with Margaret Cameron together at all.

"Charles, I'll explain all to you later," whispered Pierre.

Charles, embarrassed, looked away just as Douglas, the hotel valet-porter entered the bar, approached de Gaspé and said, "Mr. Reimer and another gentleman are waiting for you in the sitting room, Mr. de Gaspé! Cor, you ought to see the chap with 'im. Gor blimey." Then, with that a lift of his eyebrows and a twitch of his military moustache, he was gone.

"Let's go," said Pierre, gulping down the last of his gin and tonic.

As they went through the corridor from the bar into the sitting room, Kurt Reimer and his man were standing with their backs to de Gaspé and Margaret Cameron, but the new man's profile could be seen as he spoke to Reimer.

Margaret Cameron stopped in her tracks. "My God, you know who that is, don't you?" She was shocked.

So was de Gaspé. "I sure do. Every oil man in the world knows him." He took her by the arm saying, "I'll have to get out my pocket computer when we're dealing with this guy. He's incredible."

With that they went on to meet their new companions.

The luncheon went extremely well. As the luxurious food and wine were discreetly served and consumed, the new deal was presented to de Gaspé in a very British, gentlemanly fashion, adjusted on a few minor points, and agreed to by him, with Senator Cameron saying she was prepared to support the proposals.

At 2:20, de Gaspé excused himself from the table and went to his room where he placed a call to and reached first the Prime Minister in Ottawa and then the chairman of the board of Petro-Canada, whom he found this day in Winnipeg. Both men agreed to the new deal. The chairman said he would do a telephone canvas of the board and then get back to de Gaspé within two or three hours.

De Gaspé returned to the luncheon table within twenty minutes of his departure and produced the news of the Prime Minister's and chairman's reaction. There was a happy clinking of glasses in an informal spontaneous expression of delight at the new accord.

The luncheon party broke up shortly after three, with Reimer and his principal making their way back to the Dorchester, while Senator Cameron and Pierre de Gaspé returned to her room in the Stafford Hotel where, for a long, languorous hour, they "made up for lost time," as Margaret put it.

At 4:00, they were interrupted by a call from the Petro-Can's chairman of the board, who stated that the board was unanimously behind the new proposal, and in fact were quite relieved by it.

By 6:00 that evening, they were hurtling down a runway of London's Heathrow Airport in another Pan Am 747 bound for Washington and de Gaspé's meeting with Senator Weinstein in his Senate chambers. De Gaspé was well prepared for this meeting. Kurt Reimer had confirmed to him that there had indeed been two million deposited in a new numbered bank account in Switzerland.

When the steward served them their first first-class drink of the flight, Pierre turned to Margaret and said, "I think I . . . well, in all fairness, I ought to tell you about a

187

deal that Senator Weinstein has offered me if I would back-off on the Exxon takeover. When I've told you what it is, you'll know why I'm meeting him in the morning and you can tell me what you would do under the circumstances."

"Try me," replied a willing Margaret.

Washington, D.C.
Thursday, May 27, 1981, 9:30 A.M.

Senator Weinstein's attractive secretary took de Gaspé into the Senator's office, telling him that the Senator was going to be a bit late, but coffee would probably help the waiting period.

As he sipped his coffee, he took in this elegant Victorian office which was Weinstein's lair of power. The room was not large, but its richness was striking. The walls were panelled in dark, superbly crafted walnut put in place by the hands of some long-gone artisan. Books filled the shelves behind the Senator's polished mid-1800's carved desk. The brown leather covering of the chairs and chesterfield and the deep-piled rust rug blended with the reddish tone of the panelling. Not much light came in from the narrow curtained windows, but the light from a polished brass chandelier provided a sedate luster to the entire room.

The smell of cigar smoke pervaded the office, as did pictures of Senator Weinstein with famous world figures reaching back over the past twenty-five years.

This suite was indeed appropriate for a holder of one of the highest offices in the United States of America.

De Gaspé could hear the commotion in the outer office as Senator Weinstein arrived, barking orders and being asked obsequiously for instructions. Through the door of the office he came, striding quickly toward de Gaspé, a new cigar clenched firmly in his teeth. De Gaspé rose to his feet as the Senator reached for his right hand and patted him on the shoulder. "Pierre boy, it's good to see you, real good to see you. You've come just in time."

The Senator dropped de Gaspé's hand, raised his right index finger to his lips and put the tip of his left index finger to his left ear. De Gaspé got the message that the place was or might be bugged, and that extreme caution should be taken in whatever was said.

The Senator stood back and looked him in the eye. "I assume you wanted to make a statement to the press," he asked.

"I don't want to, Senator, but I think I really have no choice."

The Senator pulled his cigar out of his mouth, took de Gaspé's shoulders in both of his hands, and beamed at him, "Excellent, Pierre baby, excellent. And knowing you, I assume that you've checked on that information I gave you the other day."

De Gaspé smiled. "As your operatives have undoubtedly told you, I've just come back from Europe and, yes, I have checked, and what you told me is there, is there."

"Excellent," the Senator repeated again. He lowered his voice. "I don't think I should ask you what it is you intend to say about the situation, but I told my friends in the press you would be here this morning, and that undoubtedly you would have something important to say to them after our meeting."

With that the Senator took de Gaspé by the arm, pulled him through the office door, the outer office, and along the corridor to the Senate press conference room where it seemed to de Gaspé half the world's television cameras and reporters were waiting.

This was an environment the Senator knew and enjoyed. He left de Gaspé at the edge of the rostrum which

190

he mounted, cigar in hand. He started immediately, "Ladies and gentlemen of the press, we haven't much time because the morning session of the Senate is scheduled to begin in just a few minutes.

"As you know, Congressman Foss and I have jointly sponsored a bill to prohibit the acquisition of control of Exxon by Petro-Canada. The Weinstein/Foss bill was passed yesterday by the House of Representatives and as majority leader of the Senate, I will be introducing the Weinstein/Foss bill," he liked to hear his own name, "this morning, subject, of course, to any material change of position on the part of the Canadian government."

He waved his left arm in Pierre de Gaspé's direction. "I want to introduce to you this morning, the president of Petro-Canada. As you know, we have had discussions on this critical and serious problem of Exxon. Mr. de Gaspé has indicated to me that he has a few words to say to the press before this morning's session of the Senate. Mr. de Gaspé."

The Senator retreated from the rostrum and de Gaspé took his place, taking from his pocket a long card on which he had made some notes of the points he wanted to cover. He began quickly, the cameras whirring, microphones stacked in front of him, and eager reporters writing at full speed.

"Ladies and gentlemen," he began, "I want to say to you that in my meetings with Senator Weinstein he has been very direct and forceful in pressing his position that it is contrary to the national interest and public policy of the United States for the government of Canada or any other foreign government to gain control of Exxon Corporation or any other major American multi-national corporation. He has made it clear that he will do everything in his power to have the Weinstein/Foss bill to prohibit Petro-Canada's take-over of Exxon passed by the Senate. Having dealt with

191

this man, I am sure that he will convince his colleagues in the Senate that the bill should be passed.

"On the other hand, we in Canada have long been concerned that all of the vertically integrated oil companies operating in Canada are American owned, except BP Canada Limited, which is British owned. We believe that one of those companies should be owned by Canada, and operated in the interests of Canada. And it has been our belief that rather than nationalize, expropriate, or in some other way forcibly take over ownership or control of such a corporation in Canada, it would be more in keeping with the spirit of the way business is done on this continent, and in particular the United States, that we should attempt to buy control of such an oil corporation on the open market, thereby doing two things: number one, getting control of that corporation's operations within Canada, and number two, through the multi-national activities of the corporation, buying for ourselves a new trading, marketing, and business position in the world's markets.

"Canada's relationship with the United States, at least up until last October, has been a peaceful one, marred only by economic pushing and shoving from time to time when the great leverage and weight of the United States has been used where required to put Canada in its place."

De Gaspé turned to look at Senator Weinstein standing behind him and to his right, then back to his audience.

"Senator Weinstein has suggested to me in the most forcible of terms that Canada should withdraw its take-over bid on Exxon before he introduces his bill in the Senate, because if that bill passes, and if the President ratifies it, not only will the proposal be killed, the relationship between our two great countries will be once again greatly strained.

"He has offered that if Canada is prepared to withdraw

192

its take-over bid, then he will not introduce the Weinstein/Foss bill in the Senate this morning. I have discussed the Senator's proposal with my principals in Canada and, of course, with the Prime Minister. I am not at liberty to disclose the nature and details of those discussions except to say that the entire status of the Exxon take-over bid has been reviewed, as has been the proposal of Senator Weinstein.

"Having some idea of the Senator's belief in his own power, including his power of persuasion, there is little doubt in my mind that he now expects me to say that I have advised the Prime Minister and my principals to withdraw the Exxon bid.

"That is not what I have advised them, and therefore, that is not what I am going to say will happen.

"On the contrary, my instructions are that, subject to one material change in the offer to the shareholders of record, which change will be disclosed this afternoon, the take-over bid on Exxon is to continue."

Those words were barely out of de Gaspé's mouth when the Senator grabbed him from behind, twirled him around, stuck his face up below de Gaspé's chin and hissed, "You double-crossing bastard. I'll have you and your banana republic country for bookends."

With that Senator Jacob Weinstein of New York stormed out of the press conference.

The White House
Thursday, May 27, 1981, 2:19 P.M.

The President greeted the two men at the door of his Oval Office full of apologies. "I'm sorry to have kept you waiting, Your Excellency, but sometimes one's luncheon guests stay a little longer than anticipated—especially if they're from Exxon."

"Please, it is of no concern, Mr. President," replied the Canadian Ambassador to the United States. "It is a privilege to attend upon you on such short notice. May I introduce Pierre de Gaspé, the president of Petro-Canada."

As they shook hands, the President said, "I've certainly heard a great deal about you, Mr. de Gaspé. You've shaken the hell out of Exxon—and the whole of the United States for that matter." Then he turned, went behind his desk and motioned to his guests to be seated. As they did so, the Ambassador, Georges Charbonneau, said, "There is one other person to join us, Mr. President. He has come a long way to be here and unfortunately he has not yet arrived."

The President waved his hand, "That's all right. After all, I was good and late myself. As a matter of fact, I'm expecting Senator Weinstein and Congressman Foss any moment now. They're bringing their bill which was passed by the Senate this morning, as I'm sure you know. It's now up to me to decide what to do with it."

It was de Gaspé who spoke up. "That's the reason for the request for our meeting with you. You haven't publicly

194

disclosed your position on the Weinstein/Foss bill. We know you gave the Exxon people another chance to convince you to sign it. And then there are some new factors -"

The President broke in, "I've been on the horns of a dilemma with this one, let me assure you. As I told the Exxon people, my whole background is with the labouring class, the workers. For me to have to approve of a bill which in the long run will prevent a willing shareholder from selling his shares to a willing buyer, a bill which serves mainly to preserve the position of the Exxon management group – frankly, gentlemen, I find it damn difficult."

He shrugged. "On the other hand, here I am, a Democratic President, with a Democratic Senate and a Democratic House. Between us we're supposed to represent the will of the great American people. The Congress has spoken clearly and with a substantial majority in both houses. The Congress considers it to be contrary to the national interest and public policy that control of Exxon Corporation fall into the hands of a foreign government."

The President leaned back in his chair, "Gentlemen, reluctant as I might be in my own conscience, I'm afraid I'm going to have to approve the Weinstein/Foss bill."

As he was speaking the last few words, his intercom bell sounded and his secretary advised that the third visitor with the Canadian party had arrived. "Send him in, please," the President instructed.

The door opened instantly. President Dennis rose to move to greet the tall young man who swept elegantly into the room.

The Canadian Ambassador introduced him. "Mr. President, I have the honour to present to you another man about whom you have undoubtedly heard a great deal, His Excellency Sheik Kamel Abdul Rahman, the Minister of Oil for the Kingdom of Saudi Arabia."

The President stopped in his tracks but quickly recovered. The Sheik bowed to the President and the two men lightly shook hands.

It was an emotional moment for both, each a powerful leader among races of men who had known hatred for one another for centuries. But there would be no show, no outward trace of animosity or ingrained emotion displayed by these two men, each of them highly cultured within his own society and environment.

When they were all seated again around the desk, the President leaned forward on the edge of his chair. He was an experienced bargainer, who could sense that the crunch was coming.

He said crisply, "Well, gentlemen . . .?"

The Sheik looked at the Ambassador and then at Pierre de Gaspé. They were waiting for him to lead. "If I may, Mr. President, perhaps I can explain. I'm sure that His Excellency the Ambassador or Mr. de Gaspé will break in at any time to amplify or correct anything I have to say. I speak with the full authority of my most revered King, who as you know, Mr. President, has always held the people of the United States of America in the highest regard."

The President nodded.

"At the end of February of this year, our principal banker in Switzerland, Credit Swiss, approached my government and me concerning a request made by the Canadian government and Petro-Canada to borrow $14.5 billion for the purpose of acquiring control of Exxon Corporation. My country has had dealing for many many many years with Standard Oil of New Jersey—that is, Exxon through Aramco, the enormously profitable oil-producing firm which Exxon originally owned with others and now is mainly held by Saudi Arabia.

"The Arab oil-exporting countries such as Kuwait, Libya,

Qatar, and Abhu Dhabi and, of course, Saudi Arabia now have massive holdings of American dollars. But as a race, our characteristic is to invest those dollars as debt rather than as equity.

"The opportunity to invest $14.5 billion as debt with the security of the guarantee of the government of Canada, together with the pledge of the shares of Exxon acquired on the take-over bid as collateral – it was a unique investment opportunity for us. Therefore, without disclosing our identity, we instructed our bank to complete the negotiations and to agree to advance the required funds."

The Minister drew out a long cigarette case and said to the President, "Do you mind, sir?"

The President indicated that he did not, and in a few seconds the Sheik was puffing away, apparently relaxed and confident.

The President had not moved.

"Quite naturally we monitored closely every move made by the Canadian government and by Petro-Canada during the take-over bid. By Monday of this week it became apparent to us that the Weinstein/Foss bill would be approved by the Congress in the event that the court refused to grant the injunction that the Exxon management had applied for.

"Also, at this time, my government – that is to say, the King and his advisors – had decided that perhaps over all these years we had been too conservative, investing only in debt opportunities rather than equity. As you know, Mr. President, it is very difficult to invest large sums with reasonable security, especially when the sums I am talking of are surpluses which we now have available of at least $100 billion U.S.

"Well, we could see that one way or the other the Canadian bid would be destroyed, either by the court or in the alternative by the Congress. As we all know, the court did not uphold Exxon and therefore it was left to the Congress to act, which it has done in passing the Weinstein/Foss bill. In all this process, Mr. President, there was one unknown, or at least one unstated position, and that was yours."

The President nodded but remained silent.

"In our analysis, the Canadian proposal was doomed for failure. We felt that you, sir, would be reluctant to approve of the bill, but that for political reasons you would be forced to do so – forced unless there was some new ingredient, some new leverage, which would make it compellingly attractive for you to veto the Weinstein/Foss bill."

The Minister's monologue was interrupted by the President's intercom bell. His secretary informed him that Senator Weinstein and Representative Foss were waiting. "I'll see them shortly" was the President's terse response.

"Go on, Mr. Minister."

"Saudi Arabia and the other oil-exporting countries are now supplying the United States with about 60 per cent of its overall crude oil requirements. To have our co-operation in continuing the security of that supply, the government of the United States has in the past indicated a willingness to compromise in many areas of the relationship between the United States and the Organization of Arab Petroleum Exporting Countries.

"Perhaps it would have been enough for me to appear before you today to say that it is Saudi Arabia which is the heretofore-undisclosed financier of the main sector of the Canadian take-over bid on Exxon. Perhaps you would have decided to veto the bill on the basis of our request, and our involvement as lenders. But my King and I were of the considered view that our presence merely as disclosed lenders might not be sufficient. Accordingly, we have taken steps to put ourselves in a new position which we believe deserves your support."

Again the intercom bell. "Senator Weinstein says its urgent, Mr. President."

David Dennis sighed. "Tell him I'm aware of that and I'll be with him as quickly as I can. Please continue, Mr. Minister."

Sheik Kamel Abdul Rahman went on. "The great American oil companies, of which Exxon is but one, have been extracting and selling Saudi Arabia's crude oil throughout the world. For example, Exxon, Texaco and Standard of California are partners with my country in Aramco, the Arabian American Oil Company, and each year make huge profits from their investment. We feel that it is now time for Saudi Arabia to take the other side of the coin and do business in the United States, and to return, by way of investment, some of the enormous number of dollars that your country has been good enough to pay us for our precious oil."

The President caustically remarked, "I am also well aware that Saudia Arabia now owns 60 per cent of Aramco – 35 per cent more than it did at the beginning of 1974."

The Minister was somewhat shaken by the President's knowledge of the numbers.

"Yes, well, the day before yesterday, before Judge Amory had given his decision, I requested our bankers in Switzerland to have Mr. de Gaspé come to London to meet with me. To this point the presence of Saudi Arabia had not been disclosed to de Gaspé. I was in Geneva, at OPEC headquarters when the decision was made, so it was convenient for me to go to London." Rahman smiled, "London is a marvellous place. Such beautiful women . . .

"In any event, as a result of meetings which we held yesterday, the results of which have been confirmed by my King and our government – "

199

De Gaspé interjected, "And by the government of Canada as well."

The Minister carried on. "A new agreement has been entered into. Of course, these new arrangements can be circulated among the shareholders of record of Exxon as an amending circular to Petro-Canada's original offer which is open until June first. So I can see no problem in dealing with your Securities and Exchange Commission rules." He tamped out his cigarette butt in the ashtray on the President's desk.

"Now, Mr. President, the new arrangement is this: First, Saudi Arabia will take the place of Petro-Canada as the buyer of the shares tendered to date and will take all 59.3 per cent, which as I understand it is the amount offered as of last Sunday.

"Secondly, Saudi Arabia will continue to buy shares of Exxon Corporation on the open market until it achieves a holding of 67 per cent of all of the issued and outstanding common shares, thereby giving it total control.

"Thirdly, on the completion of the Saudi Arabian takeover of Exxon, it has been agreed that Canada will purchase from Exxon all of its issued and outstanding shares in Imperial Oil Limited, the Canadian subsidiary of Exxon Corporation, 70 per cent of the shares of which are in Exxon's hands, the balance being owned by the public."

"In this way, Canada can achieve a major national objective by owning and controlling a vertically integrated oil company which is devoted to exploration, production, refining, and merchandising petroleum products and chemicals."

President Dennis looked at de Gaspé, "This is quite a comedown for Canada, isn't it, just getting Imperial and not Exxon itself?"

The reply was quick and enthusiastic. "Not really, Mr.

President, the Exxon deal was an enormous financial commitment for the Canadian government. There is no doubt it would have strained the country's capabilities to the limit. And you may have heard that the Prime Minister has been getting a lot of flack from the Opposition and the press.

"Most of the people who have opposed the take-over bid on Exxon agree with the proposition that Petro-Canada should own and control Imperial Oil. No question about that. The financing of the acquisition is something that PetroCan itself can take care of without getting the government and the banks involved. No, Canada will be quite happy, Mr. President, to wind up in this deal with ownership of Imperial Oil, and if we can do that, the exercise of a take-over bid will have been extremely worth while. Through Imperial we can put gasoline and fuel oil on the market at low, more competitive prices and force the other majors down to a reasonable profit position which allows them an adequate return for their investors and enough money to maintain their much needed exploration programs. Speaking for Petro-Canada, I will be delighted to have Imperial's new gas and oil wells in the Mackenzie Delta as well as in the Canadian Arctic Islands and Alberta in our inventory.

"No, Mr. President, I think that, politically, the Prime Minister is absolutely delighted with the result and is really far more comfortable with the Imperial acquisition than he was with the Exxon deal."

The President nodded. "I can believe that. Also, Canada, through its deal with Saudi Arabia will have made a friend in the Arab world finally. Yes, your Prime Minister's got a good deal."

The Sheik pressed the point further. "Insofar as Saudi Arabia is concerned, Mr. President, for the first time we will be in a position to do business in your country in the same way your companies have been doing business in ours for many decades. Furthermore, this cross-fertilization of the economies of the Middle East and the United States can only serve to benefit the mutual understanding and co-operation which ought to exist between the Arab nations and the United States.

"Such new close economic ties should make it easier for both of us to strive unceasingly to maintain peace in the Middle East and to settle the Palestinian matter in an equitable and just fashion. That would be a sign of a new era, would it not, Mr. President?"

President Dennis, taut on the edge of his chair, put the question, "I hear what you're saying, Mr. Minister, and it sounds to me like either I go along with you or you and the other Arab oil countries will cut us off again just as you did after the October war in 1973!"

Rahman agreed. "That is a fair analysis, except that our cut off this time will be strictly enforced. There will be no leaks. And the interests of all of your American companies in the Middle East, including Exxon's, will be seized."

"And what if I say the United States will cut off the Arab nations in reprisal—food, machinery, medical supplies?" the President countered.

The Sheik smiled, "My dear President, cut us off if you will. We Arabs lived in the desert for 6,000 years before you people—I'm sorry—the Americans descended upon us and we can live there for another 6,000 without you. But in any event we now have a new trade relationship not only with Western Europe where you still retain a modicum of influence, but also with Japan, whose ties with us have become close and tight since the October war.

"No, Mr. President, I think this is not a time for reprisals. It is a time for doing business with your friends the Arabs who wish to have done unto them only what you have done unto yourselves."

The President stood up slowly. He paused for a moment, looked at de Gaspé and Charbonneau, then back at Sheik Kamel Abdul Rahman. The meeting was over. The President said softly, "Gentlemen, I am grateful to you for the important intelligence you have brought to me. I would appreciate it if you might leave by the side door, over to my right. Senator Weinstein and Representative Foss are waiting in the office you came through and I would like at this point to avoid a confrontation."

As his visitors stood to make their departure, the President said, "And one final thing. You should be aware that all conversations in this office are taped automatically, and that what we have said in these last few minutes is on record. I intend to play back this conversation for Weinstein and Foss before I tell them"–the President stopped and looked down at his hands which were trembling–" that I have no choice but to veto their bill."

Appendix I
A National Energy Policy for Canada

It is in the interests of the people of Canada and urgent that a comprehensive national policy for energy be forthwith created so that the goals and objectives of Canada are clearly established and that:

Such policy should deal first with crude oil, natural gas, coal and their derivatives;

It should be designed to ensure that for the foreseeable future every Canadian citizen is assured of an adequate supply of fuel oil, gasoline, and other fossil fuel products which are required to maintain the standard of living which this nation has achieved;

The national energy policy should ensure that the people of Canada have a maximum participation in the ownership of the crude oil, natural gas, coal, and their derivatives produced in Canada and that there is a maximum return to the people of Canada either through their governments or through private enterprise endeavours;

Upon the sale of the fossil fuel commodities either domestically or internationally, opportunities for Canadians to share in the proceeds be maximized through royalties, export taxes, and Canadian ownership of all unexplored gas and oil acreage in the Yukon and Northwest Territories.

In order to transport to domestic markets any and all crude oil, natural gas, coal, or other energy resources, transmission and transportation systems should be constructed in such a manner as to ensure that Canada can achieve energy self-sufficiency, while at the same time retaining the opportunity to import these vital fossil commodities should market and geopolitical conditions make it desirable to do so;

Surpluses of energy commodities should be made available to the United States;

Immediate assistance should be given to the United States in building the transportation system to move its massive volumes of natural gas from Prudhoe Bay and Alaska across Canada into the United States of America for its Midwest market.

In order to implement the national energy policy the government of Canada should work closely with an in cooperation and equality with the oil-producing and -exporting provinces of Canada rather than by confrontation and with attitudes of superiority so that the interest and positions of those provinces as clearly defined under the British North America act are respected and given full weight.

NATIONAL POLICY

1) It is the national policy that all sources of energy available within Canada are to be identified, evaluated, and estimated as to potential capacity and proven reserves.

2) The energy resources of Canada shall be conserved and shall be dedicated first to the needs and requirements of the Canadian people, provided that those amounts of energy forms which are calculated to be surplus to the needs of the Canadians within the foreseeable future may be committed for export to foreign markets.

3) Canada must achieve total energy self-sufficency at the earliest possible time and must give urgent priority and encouragement to exploration and development of its crude oil and natural gas resources including the Athabasca tarsands.

4) Canada must forthwith create transportation systems

which ensure the movement of sufficient quantities of energy in whatever form from the place or origin within Canada to the domestic market of need.

5) The national energy policy shall be both created and implemented by consultative, co-operative, joint procedures among the energy-producing governments (federal and provincial), it being the intent that both levels of government should work together as equals provided that the principles established under the British North America Act as to the resource or other jurisdictions of each level of government shall be totally respected provided further that, those rights and privileges shall be mixed and blended where it is in the interests of the people of Canada.

6) It is national policy for Canada that there be established a Canada Energy Corporation (CEC) which will work in co-operation with the National Energy Board. The purposes of the Canada Energy Corporation, which will not be a Crown corporation but which will offer shares to the Canadian public and to the provincial and federal governments, will be, among other things, as follows:

> a) CEC would undertake all crude oil and natural gas exploration in the Yukon and Northwest Territories provided that CEC will be entitled to raise exploration funds against "first rights to negotiate" for gas or oil discovered (Panarctic now has this arrangement with Tenneco and Columbia of the U.S.).
>
> b) CEC would finance and undertake the construction of the Mackenzie Valley Corridor natural gas pipeline from the Yukon-Alaska border and the Mackenzie Delta through to the U.S. border and to connect with TransCanada Pipelines for distribution throughout Canada. If no Alaska gas is committed, then a smaller line should be built to bring Mackenzie Valley gas to Canada South.

c) CEC would undertake the Mackenzie Valley Corridor pipeline construction through a wholly owned subsidiary which would raise the required construction funds 10 per cent by equity and the balance by debt financing. The division of financing would be legislated and would require a low equity input for the reason that the owners of the natural gas in the Arctic, which are all large, well-funded, U.S. multi-national corporations, and the buyers of the commodity in the United States, all have access to substantial quantities of funds and credit. Therefore the funding of construction would not be the usual "market" situation. With a $6 billion construction cost the Canadian equity required ($600 million) would be raised by public subscription and by governmental participation: no dividends would be declared nor would any interest be payable on the debt financing until such time as the gas from Prudhoe Bay and the Mackenzie Delta began to flow in the pipe.

d) CEC would be responsible for the production and sale of all crude oil and gas within its holdings and the development of systems to transport its commodities to market.

e) CEC would be empowered to undertake with the government of Alberta the creation of synthetic oil production plants in the Athabasca tarsands or to undertake such development with private enterprise.

f) CEC would be empowered to market petroleum products on a retail or wholesale basis, refine and process petroleum products. CEC would not enter the hydro electric power field except as a financing participant but would be allowed to engage with Atomic Energy of Canada Limited in the production of electricity by nuclear power.

g) CEC would undertake research and development in the search for new forms of energy.

207

7) It is national policy that in the Yukon and the Northwest Territories the privilege of exploring for crude oil and natural gas be the exclusive right of Canadians and the Canada Energy Corporation and that all exploration permits for acreage in the territories which has not yet been drilled will be revoked and the deposit monies returned to the foreign or foreign-controlled exploration companies which now hold them and all such rights shall be granted to CEC by the government of Canada.

8) It is the national policy of Canada that all steps be taken to assist the United States in obtaining access to its Prudhoe Bay and other Alaskan natural gas by the creation of a transCanada pipeline system. Commencement of construction must be early because when the crude oil pipeline from Prudhoe Bay to Valdez in Alaska is completed, the natural gas generated by the oil production at Prudhoe Bay will require that a natural gas transmission system to the United States be built within two years.

9) It is national policy that the government of Canada recognizes the rights of the native people of the Yukon and Northwest Territories and that before commencement of construction of the Mackenzie Valley natural gas pipeline a settlement should be negotiated with them.

10) It is national energy policy that the pipeline transmission corporations, being Canadian-owned regulated common carriers, be given statutory power to engage in and finance petroleum exploration and development within Canada.

11) It is national policy that exhaustive research be mounted into all possible modes of transporting fossil fuels from the Canadian Arctic Islands having due regard to the delicate eco-system of that region.

12) It is the national policy of Canada that there be established an authority to have power to exercise an over-

view of the domestic and international marketing, distribution, and pricing for all crude oil and natural gas and their derivatives produced in Canada; and that the members of such authority be comprised of nominees of the oil- and gas-producing governments (federal and provincial); and that such body be named the Canadian Organization of Petroleum Exporting Governments (COPEG).

13) The price to be paid by Canadians for their domestic forms of energy shall be related to the cost of production of those resources within Canada and shall not be related to world market prices: provided that energy forms for export shall be priced in accordance with the world market. The share of the people of Canada of the price paid for energy commodities shall be maximized by means of ownership, royalties, and taxes.

14) COPEG would be responsible for creating and implementing such programs as may be necessary for the allocation, distribution, pricing, and rationing of gasoline and fuel oil.

15) The National Energy Board would retain its historic role and powers except where such powers are provided to COPEG: and the NEB shall be advisory to COPEG.

IMPLEMENTING POLICIES

1) A pipeline to deliver western crude oil to Montreal refineries should be built forthwith by Canada using government funds; and a transportation system for western crude oil and refined products to the Maritime provinces should be designed and built.

2) Emergency plans should be prepared to move gasoline and fuel oil from Ontario refineries into Quebec and the Maritimes.

3) The price of western crude should be allowed to rise

when the federal export impost is removed provided that the price to which it is permitted to rise for domestic consumption is limited to an amount which reflects the Canadian oil industry's stated need for funds to enable it to continue its exploration and development (the industry says that western crude production will cease by 1984 unless new finds are made); and provided further that the oil industry gives a firm commitment that the funds obtained by the price rise will be used for exploration and development.

4) Special tax incentives should be provided immediately for the development of the Athabasca tarsands.

5) Comprehensive steps be taken on a nationwide basis to encourage and, if necessary, direct that the consumption of fossil fuels be reduced, especially by automobile users.

6) A national energy conference of first ministers should be held immediately to:

    a) resolve energy disputes between the federal and provincial governments.

    b) negotiate and create a national energy policy for Canada.

    c) resolve the matter of domestic and export pricing of crude oil and natural gas

    d) establish the Canadian Organization of Petroleum Exporting Governments and to provide COPEG with terms of reference and such legislated authority as may be necessary.

    e) prepare short- and long-term goals and strategy to ensure that Canada's energy relationship with the United States is responsive to the escalating energy crisis in that nation.

Appendix II
Hansard, Thursday, November 20, 1980

THE PRIME MINISTER'S SPEECH OUTLINING THE CONCEPT OF A
MOBILE HOUSE OF COMMONS.

Mr. Speaker, when this nation was created and this Confederation established in 1867, it was appropriate and indeed it was mandatory that there be a capital. That capital was Ottawa, and it was mandatory and appropriate for all Honourable Members of this House in that day to proceed to Ottawa from their constituencies for the sittings of this House, knowing full well that apart from the benefit of communications by post, carried from their homes and the ridings which they represented to Ottawa by horse, carriage, rail, and often by vessel, there would be no opportunity to communicate with the home riding or other parts of Canada as it then was, and there would be little or no way of returning quickly to one's home area for a short visit.

Therefore, for all Members and Senators the Parliament Buildings at Ottawa were the one and only place in which it was practical for the House of Commons to meet. And so it has remained over the past one hundred and fourteen years a requirement that all who have business to do with Parliament whether from the Pacific Coast, the Atlantic Coast, or indeed, from the shores of the Arctic Ocean, they must come to Ottawa. Decisions are made by the House of Commons affecting all of those places by men and women of this House, many of whom have never seen those regions, or been among the people who populate them.

Mr. Speaker, in the almost twelve decades since Confederation there have been changes in the world the like of which mankind has never before seen.

211

We now have the magic of television, of computers, of the telephone, of the telex system. We can transmit pictures and pages of print electronically. We can communicate with all parts of the world by fantastic space satellites. We can move in massive jet aircraft from place to place throughout this country in short, almost magically short, periods of time. We have automobiles which carry us from place to place as matters of mecessity. We have radio, trucks, and a host of other transportation and communications devices which have made this country small, reachable – a place in which close contact can be maintained at all times.

While I do not propose that what I am about to say should be actually done, I do say to you, Mr. Speaker, that theoretically – I am sure it would never be done for obvious reasons – we could take every Member of this House and every Deputy Minister and put them all in one huge Boeing 747 and transport all of them to any major city in Canada within a matter of four hours at the outside.

Mr. Speaker, I am not proposing that the House of Commons move across Canada as a single unit, first of all because we would be fighting over which direction in which to fly and, secondly, if the aircraft were to crash, there would be a slight vacuum created.

One of the prime concerns of this government is to maintain every possible strength of national unity which can be achieved. We have been racked in this country by regional stresses and claims by the rising power of the provinces in their confrontations with the Federal Government, matters of regional disparity and some issues which from time to time, Mr. Speaker, have made it a real question as to whether or not Canada in its current form of Confederation would be able to survive.

212

Mr. Speaker, the time has come when the House of Commons, with all of the transportation and communications facilities available to it, ought properly to sit and do business for short periods of time in the major regional cities of Canada.

In this way, all Members of the House will demonstrate to the people of the local area in which the House is sitting that they have an interest in the people of that region and their problems and that the Members of Parliament are available to those people. Furthermore, it may well be that for many Members of this House a visit to a given city of Canada might well be that Member's first visit to that region.

For these reasons, Mr. Speaker, I propose that the House of Commons sit in Edmonton, the capital city of the Province of Alberta, for the period commencing Tuesday, March 3rd, 1981, and for a six-week period thereafter, and that the House should sit at Quebec City for a similar period in the fall of 1981 and in Yellowknife in the spring of 1982 and in other cities in the spring and fall of each following year.

This proposal has been reviewed and approved by a committee comprised of all parties which has worked out the arrangements for accommodation and for conversion of an appropriate arena or other structure in Edmonton into a temporary House of Commons.